Books by Jody Hedlund

Young Adult: The Lost Princesses Series
Always: Prequel Novella
Evermore
Foremost
Hereafter

Young Adult: Noble Knights Series
The Vow: Prequel Novella
An Uncertain Choice
A Daring Sacrifice
For Love & Honor
A Loyal Heart
A Worthy Rebel

The Bride Ships Series
A Reluctant Bride
The Runaway Bride

The Orphan Train Series
An Awakened Heart: A Novella
With You Always
Together Forever
Searching for You

The Beacons of Hope Series
Out of the Storm: A Novella
Love Unexpected
Hearts Made Whole
Undaunted Hope
Forever Safe
Never Forget

The Hearts of Faith Collection
The Preacher's Bride
The Doctor's Lady
Rebellious Heart

The Michigan Brides Collection
Unending Devotion
A Noble Groom
Captured by Love

Historical
Luther and Katharina
Newton & Polly

Always

JODY HEDLUND

NORTHERN LIGHTS PRESS

NORLAND

HIGHLANDS

HIGHLAND CONVENT

ST. CUTHBERT'S

IRON HILLS

STEFFORD

MIDDLETON

EVERLY

WEST MOORLAND

EASTERN PLAINS

EAST SEA

MERCIA

CANNOCK

CISTERN BOGS

LANGLEY

CRESS RIVER

DELSWORTH

CENTRAL HEATHLANDS

SMITHTIDE

WELLMONT RUINS

INGLEWOOD FOREST

WARWICK

GREAT ISLE

Chapter 1

Felicia

"Another sip, Your Majesty," I pleaded, holding out the golden chalice of raspberry-leaf tea. I tried to quell my shaking so I wouldn't spill the liquid that was supposed to slow the bleeding but hadn't yet.

The queen clamped her lips closed to fend off another scream. Against the feather bolster and pillow beres, the beautiful woman was as pale as the linen sheets she lay upon. Her eyes were glassy, and her blond hair had come loose from its plait and now lay in tangled waves, damp with perspiration.

"The babe is finally coming." The head midwife spoke calmly from the footboard of the large canopied bed. "I need more chamomile massage oil."

One of the other ladies rushed across the chamber to do the midwife's bidding in preparation for the next royal son or daughter. With so few ladies remaining after the evacuation of the palace, we'd all worked tirelessly during the past eighteen hours that the queen had been in labor, attempting to ease her distress as best we could.

Although my stomach roiled with squeamishness every time I glimpsed the bloody sheets the midwives kept taking away, I was thankful I hadn't left Delsworth Castle with the other ladies-in-waiting as the queen had urged. After all the kindness she'd shown to me in the year I'd lived at the royal residence, aiding in her travail was the least I could do in return.

"Push, Your Majesty," the head midwife said, her voice commanding and soothing at the same time.

The queen fumbled for something to grasp. I rapidly placed the chalice on the bedside table and enfolded her hand in mine.

"You are a strong and brave woman." I bent in closer and smoothed loose strands off her forehead. "You can do this."

"No, Felicia. I cannot." She gasped, and the muscles in her neck and face bulged with the strain of her labor.

"If anyone can do this," I said softly, "it is you."

And I believed it with all my heart. Her Royal Majesty Dierdal Aurora Leandra, Queen of Mercia, was truly the kindest, noblest, and most gracious woman I knew. While she required impeccable conduct from her ladies-in-waiting, she always expected more of herself than of anyone else.

Even during the past fortnight while an invading army had overrun the capital city of Mercia and besieged the castle, the queen had maintained the strictest order among the few of us ladies who were still with her. She'd kept us all too busy to think about the enemy surrounding the moat and fortified walls.

When the battering rams had grown loud, she requested we play our music louder. When the smoke from the firebombs penetrated the inner rooms of the keep, she had more fans and incense brought in. When the reports of skirmishes on the ramparts had been unfavorable, she added more prayer hours to our schedule.

Yesterday, after a young soldier came with news that the king had been injured during a particularly fierce battle on the wall, the queen had remained focused and strong—at least outwardly. Privately, I had no doubt she was worried about her husband, and I couldn't keep from wondering if the report of the king's injury had caused her to go into labor. The midwives hadn't seemed overly anxious about the arrival of the child a few weeks early, especially since the queen's abdomen had shown the babe to be of a good size.

Now the queen strained, holding her breath and squeezing my hand for so long, I started to panic. "Breathe, Your Majesty," I urged.

Her lips turned blue and quivered before she finally sucked in a sharp gasp of air. A tiny wail rent the air. A newborn wail.

Tears pricked my eyes—tears of both joy and relief. The childbirth was over.

Around the room came excited murmurs and clapping from the other ladies, followed by the midwife's triumphant pronouncement. "You've delivered a healthy princess, Your Majesty."

The queen dropped her head into the pillow beres and bolster, her body limp, her face more ashen. As her lashes fell, I caught a glimpse of sadness before a tear escaped down her cheek. The birth of a child ought to be a time of joy, not despair. But with her husband injured and the city besieged, perhaps the rejoicing would come later.

With a start and sharp gasp, the queen sat forward, clutching my hand again. Another contraction wracked her body, this one tighter and more powerful than any that had come before. Though the regal woman had endured her travail silently thus far, a chilling scream escaped her lips as if torn from her by force.

Every conversation and movement came to a halt, and all eyes turned upon her.

The midwife's brow furrowed, adding wrinkles to her already aged face. Her intelligent eyes flashed with worry that sparked fear inside me. She examined the queen again, and her eyes widened with surprise. "I do believe the queen is about to have a second babe."

Twins? Gasps rippled around the chamber.

For an endless moment, the queen struggled to bring another new life into the world. Veins in her temples protruded, pulsing and pounding ribbons of blue. After the tiny squalling cries of a second babe finally rose to greet us, the queen collapsed against her pillow beres once more.

"Another princess," the other ladies whispered reverently.

"I need my stitching kit," the midwife called, handing the care of the infant over to her attendant. Instead of triumph, urgency edged the midwife's voice, which only stirred the anxiety in my chest.

The queen's grip in mine melted away. Her lashes fluttered up to reveal eyes so glazed I wasn't sure she could focus. Nevertheless, she shifted her gaze to my hovering face.

I snatched up the chalice of raspberry-leaf tea and lifted it to her lips.

She shook her head, turning her mouth away. "Felicia?"

"Yes, Your Majesty. I am here."

"Take my babes." Her voice was halting and breathless.

The nursemaids were already in the process of bathing and swaddling the first of the newborns in the nursery next to the queen's chambers and would soon be doing the same for the second. The wet nurse was ready and waiting. I could do nothing for the princesses, but I couldn't tell that to the queen, not in her state. The best course was to agree with whatever she asked and pacify her as much as I could. "Where would you like me to take the babes, Your Majesty?"

"Flee from Delsworth," the queen continued with gasping breaths.

Flee from Delsworth? Was the fighting going so poorly the queen feared defeat?

"My crown." She glanced sideways at the pedestal table on the opposite side of the bed where the crown sat upon a black velvet cushion. "Take out two rubies, one for each twin."

I nodded, not sure how I would do so but determined to promise anything to this woman who'd welcomed me so warmly into her home.

"You must find Constance," she rasped.

The three-year-old crown princess Constance had already been removed from the Delsworth fortress several weeks ago when King Francis ordered the evacuation. That's when most of the other ladies-in-waiting had left with as many of the castle staff and courtiers who could be spared. The entourage journeyed by barges up the Cress River to another royal dwelling in Everly, one of the Iron Cities. The king had wanted the queen to leave, but she'd already taken to her bed with early labor pains and had been in too much discomfort to travel.

At the time, the relocation had been only a precaution. We'd heard rumors King Ethelwulf of Warwick was on the move, that he'd hired mercenaries from the continent—toughened Dane warriors as well as lethal brown-skinned Saracens. However, we hadn't expected King Ethelwulf to attack by sea so swiftly and with so much power. Certainly, we'd never believed he could overcome the massive seaport fortress that King Francis and Queen Dierdal had made their primary residence. Built of granite from the Highlands, the outer wall was ten feet thick.

"Please, Felicia," the queen whispered, her lips thin, her voice barely audible. "I trust you more than any other to see that my daughters are safe."

Trust me? Why?

At seventeen, I was one of the youngest ladies-in-waiting, and I wasn't anyone special. In fact, the queen knew I was more of a misfit because I disdained the noble courtship process—the system whereby each family sent one of their daughters to the royal court to be matched with a young man chosen as the heir of his own family.

The process of singling out a son and daughter was fraught with complications that had torn apart many families, including my own, in ways that were irreparable. My brothers had fought bitterly in a rivalry to become the chosen son who would eventually inherit our family's Avington estate and fortune. Even though Charles had prevailed and gone to court and was now betrothed, my brothers hadn't reconciled and likely never would. Furthermore, my two older sisters resented me—the chosen daughter.

Now, after almost a year at the palace, I scorned the courtship process even more. I felt like a decorative object on a pedestal under intense scrutiny, with men constantly surveying my waist-length sable curls, every inch of my smooth complexion that Mother had worked so hard to keep unblemished, and my slender body that was honed to perfection.

I might not have been the most beautiful young noblewoman at court, but I'd been groomed for this existence my entire life and should have felt privileged. But my dissatisfaction had only grown. Although I'd tried to keep it from the queen, she'd been too perceptive. She'd coaxed me into explaining my reservations about court life and had listened attentively as she always did.

I hadn't expected her to rise up and revolutionize a system that most of the aristocracy believed kept our noble lineages strong and flourishing. Nevertheless, I had felt better for sharing honestly with the queen, and I admired her all the more for her willingness to understand my frustration.

Her words had stayed with me. "Ofttimes we cannot change the entire direction of a route already set in motion. But we can do our small part to shift the path one degree at a time."

"What will your part be, Felicia?" she'd asked.

I hadn't known how to answer her. I still didn't. But I had been attempting to discover my purpose ever since.

Even so, I couldn't imagine why she would trust me with her newborn babes. Not when other, more important, stronger people could surely keep her daughters safer than I could. After all, how would I be able to leave the castle? Not when King Ethelwulf's mighty army surrounded it. Slipping out of the walled fortress and past the enemy would have been hard enough by myself. But carrying two newborn babes—and royal heirs no less? Impossible. King Ethelwulf's jealousy, greed, and ruthlessness preceded him. He wouldn't willingly allow any of the royal family to escape. Besides, if I somehow managed to smuggle the babes away, where would I go? How would I provide for them?

"Felicia," the queen whispered so faintly I had to bend low. "You can do this. For me. For my daughters. For all of us."

From the end of the bed, the midwife shouted for more supplies, her voice insistent and panicked. The queen held my gaze, and her eyes cleared of the haze of pain, revealing the strong, intelligent, and kind woman I had come to know. A glimmer in the depths told me she believed in me and thought I was strong and intelligent too.

"I will try to save them, Your Majesty," I said, but not without trepidation.

"Do you vow it?"

"I do."

She lifted her hand from the bed. It shook terribly and seemed to cost her the last ounce of remaining energy. I bent and placed three kisses there, as was the custom when making a vow, in turn pledging my allegiance, my loyalty, and my life.

Although I had not expected such a heavy task to

befall me, nor to make such a pledge, I pressed a fourth and final kiss against the queen's hand—the seal of my vow to her, a promise upon a promise, the assurance that her trust in me was well-placed.

She gave a gentle, almost imperceptible squeeze before loosening her grip and dropping her hand. I kept my head bent in servitude, but also because I didn't want her to see the fear and uncertainty in my eyes when I lifted my countenance.

Her hand slipped off the bed and dangled limply in midair.

Around me, the midwives called frantic orders, and the other ladies rushed to fulfill the commands. "I have to find a way to stop the bleeding!" the head midwife said, no longer attempting to mask her fear. "Lady Felicia, give the queen more of that tea. Now!"

I picked up the chalice but halted halfway to the queen's lips. Her eyes were closed, her lashes fanned across her pale skin. Everything about her body lay silent and still. Her lips were slightly parted as if she'd spoken her last words and taken her last breath.

My fingers began to shake so violently that some of the tea sloshed over the rim and splashed onto the sheet. A crimson spot spread like a fast-growing web, its layers tangling and dividing and encroaching as if to catch its prey.

I took a quick step back, unable to tear my eyes from the dead queen. She'd known she was dying. She'd known a silky snare was growing that would soon catch us all in its tangle. And she'd known I would need to race to save the princesses.

I prayed to God the Father, Son, and Holy Ghost I wasn't too late.

Chapter 2

LANCE

THE GRIT OF SMOKE AND SWEAT LINED EVERY CREVICE OF MY FACE, the metallic taste of blood lingering against my lips and on my tongue. Whether my own or the splattered lifeblood of my latest kill, I could not distinguish.

The sword sheathed at my side clanked against my chain mail on one side. My flail swung from the other. My leather soldier boots slapped the hallway floor in tempo to the frantic thud of my heart. Breathless, I reached the king's chamber and saluted the two soldiers standing guard before I identified myself by touching the silver boar badge affixed to my chest. The insignia symbolized the bravery and honor I'd earned that set me apart as a retainer in the king's private army. The honor allowed me extra privileges and a higher income I eagerly sent home to my mother and siblings.

But tonight, at this moment, the order from my commander to deliver the latest battle news to the king was not a privilege I'd wanted to have. Not when the news was so devastating. And not when I was tasked with secreting the king to safety—a move our noble ruler would surely resist.

The soldiers at the door regarded me with frightened eyes. Their gazes darted past me to the passageway, to the screams of torture and terror that were no longer contained to the castle walls but drew closer with each passing minute.

"Lance of the Elite Guard. I must see the king at once."

The soldiers parted and opened the door for me. The room was dimly lit and hazy from the smoke of a dozen incense pots and thick with the bitter odor of bloodwort. I homed in on King Francis lying unmoving on his luxurious bed. A physician pressed leeches against the king's already bruised arm for another bloodletting. At the clank of my armor and heavy thud of my boots upon my entrance, the king lifted his head and attempted to push up to his elbows, but immediately dropped back with a groan.

Heedless of the courtiers, clerks, physicians, clergy, and others of the royal retinue that crowded the chamber, I strode to the end of the raised bed, lowered myself to one knee, and bent my head. I wanted to blurt out the news and tell everyone in the room to take cover before the keep was captured, but even in the direst of circumstances, I couldn't break the code of conduct that required the king to acknowledge me before I could stand and speak.

"Lance? Is that you?" The king spoke in a stilted voice, each word laced with pain.

"Aye, Your Majesty."

"What tidings do you have?"

I stood and stared at his chest, for I was unworthy to look directly into the eyes of any royal or nobleman. Even though I was one of the lucky few to better my station, I was still not and never would be equal.

"Your Majesty," I started, but my attention snagged on the mound of bandages wrapped around the king's torso. A stain of blood had seeped through a spot beneath his rib cage. I'd heard the king had been wounded yesterday during a particularly fierce skirmish on the west wall, but I hadn't realized how severely.

A chill skittered up my backbone.

Aye, I greatly admired the king for his willingness to fight alongside his noble knights and lords. He'd modeled determination, courage, and honor to face the enemy rather than sending his men out to do so in his stead.

Yet the king was neither as strong nor as young as his elite warriors who'd been specially chosen for our physical prowess, strength, and speed. At six feet two inches, I'd barely met the required height for the king's army. Many others were taller and stockier. Most, like me, had spent many years as a page, then squire, with intense training both physically and mentally before being accepted to serve the king.

If the strongest warriors in Mercia had failed to keep Ethelwulf's army from overrunning the walled city that spread out as the footstool of the royal residence, then the king shouldn't have been fighting.

But it was too late for regrets. All we could do now was to ensure the king's safety.

"Your Majesty," I repeated. "Ethelwulf has breached the castle walls. The battle has moved to the bailey."

The news apparently came as no surprise to the king or his council.

"Is the keep secured?" asked a stately, gray-haired man standing closest to the king's bed. He wore a golden livery collar that announced he was the king's most trusted advisor.

I bowed my head toward the man before responding. "The doors are sealed, but Ethelwulf's contingency of Saracen warriors will be inside erelong."

A murmuring rippled among the men, their faces reflecting their fear. Legends abounded regarding the Saracens, stories brought back from merchant marines who'd encountered the desert warriors and claimed they could sneak up and slash with their curved scimitars, killing their victims faster than a flying arrow.

Not only had Ethelwulf managed to hire the Saracens as mercenaries in his army, but he also had a squad of the vicious big-boned Danes of Viking descent. While I'd brought down a number of the giantlike warriors single-handedly during the course of the fighting, I had not done so easily.

"We must aid the king to safety," I said to the king's trusted advisor before returning my attention to the king. "Your Majesty, you must leave the castle immediately."

The king closed his eyes. "I shall not make it."

I looked to the king's advisor, silently pleading for his permission to hasten the king away. The man nodded grimly before motioning to the two guards who stood on either side of the footboard. "Assemble a litter to carry the king."

The room became a hustle of activity as the men prepared to leave. Of course, we had plans for an emergency evacuation. We'd just never expected we would have need to implement those plans. Nor had we expected to do so when the king was so injured, he could hardly move.

I wasted no time now in grabbing the king's cloak and

bending near to assist the others in lifting him onto a pallet—the same bloodstained board that had been used to transport him away from the battle.

"No!" He raised a hand in protest of my effort to move him.

"Please, Your Majesty," I said with bowed head. "We have little time to spare."

"I shall—only—slow the escape." Each of the king's words came out tight and stilted.

I couldn't argue with him. I'd been told the secret tunnel that burrowed far underground was not easy for a healthy man to traverse, much less one so wounded. It went beneath the moat and led to a highly secretive exit no one knew about—except the king and the magnate of his elite army. And now me and my fellow knight, Baldric.

Of course, once we opened the tunnel, the enemy would discover the hidden passageway soon enough, but the hope was that we could get the king, queen, and the remaining civilians and servants out before our enemy learned of our evacuation plans and attempted to follow us.

"You have no need to worry, Your Majesty," I reassured. "I'll get you to safety and will carry you myself if need be."

The king sucked in a breath and grasped his injured side. I tried to wait patiently for his pain to subside, but with every passing second, we lost precious time. Perhaps I would have to scoop him up and run, heedless of his protests and the pain it cost him.

"The queen," he stammered through a shuddering breath.

"Another elite guard has gone to aid her escape—"

The chamber door banged open, cutting off my

words. Every muscle in my body tensed with alertness, and I spun as I unsheathed both my sword and dagger, ready to impale the newcomer if necessary.

At the sight of Baldric's familiar towering frame, I lowered my weapons. What was he doing here? He was supposed to be helping the queen.

He tossed back his chain mail hood, revealing the triple strands of warrior braids on his scalp that converged at the back of his neck and were tied together with a leather strip. The style was identical to mine and to all the men who served in the king's guard, except my hair hadn't darkened with age but had remained a light golden wheat.

Baldric's face was red with perspiration and stricken with grief. "The queen is dead," he gasped. "From childbirth."

At the sickening news, my stomach clenched. The king stilled, and the room grew silent enough that the shouts and cries of battle in the bailey rose up as an urgent reminder. We had to leave. Now. No matter how awful the queen's death was, my mission was to save the king. And I had to do it at any cost.

I slipped my hands underneath the king to transfer him to the waiting litter, but he resisted by grabbing my arm.

"The newborn babe?" he asked Baldric in an eerily calm voice.

"Twin daughters," my comrade replied with a furtive glance over his shoulder. Were the Saracens even now invading the residence? If so, we had even less time than I thought to make our escape.

The king fumbled deep within his pocket and pulled out a leather pouch that was attached tightly to a girdle underneath his garments. Only when he removed his hand from my arm did I realize he'd left a handprint on my sleeve—a handprint of blood. His own. My sights dropped to the bandage below his rib cage and the ever-widening spot of blood, then to his blood-slickened fingers unable to loosen the pouch.

I touched the bag. "May I, Your Majesty?" I asked as gently as I could, wishing I had time for words of comfort. But I'd been trained to think and act rapidly, and that required cutting myself off from emotions that might cloud my judgment or slow me down.

"The knot is tight," he said as he let me have access to the leather straps, "as I have never been without this bag since the day I became king."

With a flick of my knife, I slashed the pouch open, allowing the king to reach inside and remove a bundle wrapped in black velvet and tied with several pieces of twine.

My skin prickled with the feeling the enemy was drawing near, an instinct I'd learned not to ignore. We didn't have time for the king to untie this bundle too.

As though sensing my urgency, the king pressed the item into my hand. "Guard this with your life. It is for my daughters and will help them one day to reclaim the throne." He gave a sharp gasp and reached for his side. His gaze met mine before I could look away. His eyes were filled with immeasurable sadness and loss. But a spark of determination burned in the depths. "Save them, Lance."

"I'll save you too—"

"No!" Although everything within me demanded I drop my gaze and told me I was dishonoring the king with my familiarity, he held me captive with a sudden fierceness in his expression. "Keep the princesses safe until the time is right."

I nodded, hoping the move would reassure him. I'd do as he asked, but I wouldn't abandon him. When I'd joined the elite guard, I pledged to serve the king with my life. I would die for him if need be. I couldn't leave this room without him.

"Go now," he said, as though reading my mind. "It is too late for me and for the rest of the people here. But not for the princesses. Not if you help them."

With that, his eyes rolled back in their sockets, and he released a long gasping breath. Then he didn't move. He simply stared at the canopy overhead, his eyes wide and unblinking.

My wildly beating heart stumbled to a halt.

He was gone. I'd seen enough dead men to know.

A piercing scream wafted from a corridor somewhere in the castle, the kind of tortured scream that told me the Saracens had made it into the residence, likely through an open window or even a garderobe hole.

I closed the king's eyes. Then I quickly kissed the tips of my forefingers three times and pressed them to his heart. He'd been right. I was too late to save him. But I could honor his last wish or die trying.

Around me, the king's chamber succumbed to a mass of confusion as the realization of the king's death began to penetrate the retinue. I tucked the velvet bundle into an inner pocket under my chain mail and at the same time crossed to Baldric. "We must hurry to the queen's chambers." Baldric nodded curtly, and I followed him out of the king's private rooms down the long, deserted hallway.

"What shall be done with the rest of the nobility and

castle staff?" Baldric asked.

If the enemy had already infiltrated the fortress, we had no time to institute the evacuation plan. The king had known it, and Baldric knew it as well. While I had no wish to leave everyone behind, I had to make the princesses my first priority. "We'll pray that if they surrender and pledge fealty to Ethelwulf, that he will show them mercy." At least those who weren't killed by the Saracens could pledge fealty.

"I will defend you until you are safely away with the princesses," Baldric said. "Then I'll return to protect those who remain."

The hairs on the back of my neck rose even as a *whoosh* of putrid air assaulted me. A faint line formed in the arched doorway of a nearby alcove. "To your left!" I warned Baldric as I drew both of my weapons and ducked.

Talon-like fingers raked the air where my face had been only a second earlier. A shadowy figure screeched in anger at missing me but spun like a sandstorm. I pivoted and brought my sword down reflexively, a lunge that only anticipated the Saracen's next move. If my instincts were wrong, I'd pay with the curved scimitar embedded into my chest digging through my flesh.

My sharp double-edged blade severed something. I didn't wait to see what but immediately thrust my dagger upward. It connected too. A fading scream told me my blades had done their job on my opponent. I spun halfway with my bloodied sword and aimed it for the back of the Saracen who had sprung upon Baldric. At my thrust, the thin wraith froze in midair and then crumpled to the floor next to his companion.

Baldric jumped back, his weapons at the ready. But the two bodies on the hallway floor lay motionless. Blood pooled almost black around the brown-skinned men wearing robes that had likely once been white but were now grimy and tattered. The stench of their filthy garments and unwashed bodies was offensive even for a seasoned soldier like me. But I couldn't complain since their odor had alerted me to their presence and given me the split second I'd needed to react.

The outstretched hand of one of the Saracens revealed long fingernails filed to deadly sharp points. Fresh blood covered them.

I glanced to Baldric. He shook his head, answering the question before I could ask. If he hadn't been injured, then we had to pray the blood didn't belong to the newborn princesses.

We both started forward at the same time, running, our feet pounding in urgency. The queen's chambers were located on the opposite side of the keep, strategically positioned so that if the king was besieged first, the queen could still make her escape.

"There." Baldric nodded to a half-open door.

I bolted ahead of him, my speed exceeding his. As I burst into the chamber, the weeping of the women surrounding the queen's bed turned into frightened gasps and cries of alarm.

In one wide glance, I took in the pale, lifeless face of the queen centered in her large canopied bed, a noblewoman brushing the long golden hair and another helping to style it. Still another was laying out an elegant gown, clearly intending to dress the queen in preparation for her funeral. The midwives were in the process of cleaning up towels, sheets, and tiny glass bottles that had likely contained every herbal decoction that had ever been created for child birthing.

All eyes now focused on Baldric and me, and filled with terror. I didn't have the heart to tell them we were the least of their concerns. That the king was dead now too. That Ethelwulf would be in control of the castle by the end of the night. That without the king and queen, Ethelwulf would finally lay claim to Mercia. That they would become his vassals—if he allowed them to live.

"The princesses?" I asked even as I began to wind through the room toward a door I assumed would lead to the nursery.

One of the midwives, sagging from both exhaustion and dejection, pointed toward the inner door. "That way."

I wasted no time, not even with words of thanks. I threw open the door to find a smaller chamber, one that had been decorated for a newborn babe with an elaborately carved crib, light-colored tapestries and blankets, cushioned chairs positioned near the hearth, and a wardrobe displaying an assortment of infant clothing.

Two maidservants knelt in front of leather satchels. At the sight of Baldric and me, their whispered chattering came to a stop. Their eyes widened, revealing both confusion and fright.

"I've come for the princesses," I said in a tone that brooked no arguing.

At my pronouncement, a young woman stepped forward. I didn't need an introduction to know she was of noble birth. Her beauty gave that away. Younger than the ladies I'd seen in the queen's chamber, this woman had long dark hair, as lustrous and rich as prized mink. Her face was perfectly symmetrical, her cheekbones high, her chin petite and delicate, her nose elegant. Thick lashes framed her wide eyes. I surveyed her face in an instant then focused on the opal button at her collarbone holding her cloak closed.

"The princesses are gone," she said. But even as she motioned at me to leave, one of the satchels on the floor echoed with a tiny cry.

In two strides, I was beside the bag, staring down at a tiny swaddled infant tucked securely inside amidst a bed of soft blankets and clothing. Her red face contorted with what appeared to be anger. Could a babe be angry? About what?

The infant gave another squall louder than the last.

I stepped back, uneasiness swirling around my gut. I could handle the most vicious of Saracens and the toughest Dane. But manage a newborn babe? What had I gotten myself into?

"You must be away," Baldric urged behind me. "Before you're discovered."

Once again, my training overrode my emotions. I grabbed the satchel, but before my fingers could close around the handles, the young noblewoman unsheathed a knife from under her cloak and pointed it at me. "Unhand the bag and I will do you no harm."

Her fingers trembled, a clear sign she'd never had to use a knife before, that she wouldn't know how to hurt me with it even if she tried. And she apparently didn't know I could have knocked it out of her hand the moment she unsheathed it and slit her throat in the same motion.

"Your ladyship," I said, trying to keep the irritation from my voice. "Before his death, the king tasked me with taking the princesses to safety."

"And the queen tasked me likewise."

"Now that I'm here, I release you from your duty."

"I release you from yours." Her tone turned to iron. She had authority over me, and I had none over her. And we both knew it.

I couldn't stop myself from lifting my gaze to hers, even though such direct eye contact was disrespectful. Perhaps my defiance came from having already dismissed etiquette with the king. Whatever the case, I found myself peering into a pair of stunning eyes—a striking green that rivaled pure emeralds. They were arresting, almost mesmerizing in their beauty. But there was something deeper lurking beneath the surface, something that told me this woman wouldn't be easily swayed from her mission.

Chapter 3

Felicia

The young knight stared at me much too boldly. In fact, I couldn't remember the last time a king's guard or any servant had ever dared to look at me. I ought to rebuke him, perhaps even report him. But at the cry that came from the satchel, I shifted my attention.

"How long before the sleeping tonic takes effect?" I asked as I took several more bottles of milk from the wet nurse. I'd already packed half a dozen into the bottom of one satchel and needed a supply for the other princess.

"A few more minutes, your ladyship," answered the maidservant who'd administered the sleeping aid. "Already the older princess is asleep. The younger princess will be soon enough."

The queen had previously chosen several names in preparation for either a boy or girl. I'd taken the top two girl names from her list. I'd decided to call the firstborn Maribel and the other twin Emmeline. Then I'd burned the list and decided I would tell no one the names, at least until I knew the princesses were safe.

I'd had to push aside my feelings of guilt for naming them without a priest and without the proper ceremony. But I was rushed to ensure I left with the necessities, much less the proprieties. Thankfully, the male servant I'd called had been able to take two rubies from the queen's crown, and I'd tucked them away in my pocket.

"I've no time to wait for medicine to set in," the knight said with a sharp glance at his companion, who was taller and wider. The two wore long hauberks as well as hoods and mantles of the same tightly riveted metal rings. Bright crimson splatters mingled with darker brown, adding to the filth that coated them and lined their faces. Only then did I notice their drawn swords slathered in fresh blood. I'd heard the screams within the castle and had prayed the enemy wasn't already inside. Had I finally run out of time?

My heartbeat pattered with the same apprehension that had been my companion since the queen garnered my vow.

"Retrieve the rest of the bottles," I ordered the nearest servant, who rushed into the antechamber where the wet nurse had been busy pouring milk into the bottles as rapidly as she could. "I need more blankets," I said to another maid.

Before I could stop the knight, he picked up both satchels. "I'm taking the babies now." Then without waiting for my approval, he stalked from the room, his companion following him.

"Halt this instant," I called after him in what I hoped was my most severe and haughty tone. But he kept going, speeding his pace into a jog.

I grabbed the remaining blankets and bottles from the servants, wrapped them together, and then dashed to catch up with the knights. They were in the hallway and had started running.

"Stop!" I called, my voice echoing in the eerily empty passageway.

The first of the young knights—the one carrying the satchels—tossed a glance over his shoulder. It was filled with irritation, the same I'd witnessed before. "Stay in the queen's chambers. You'll be safest there."

"I shall not abandon my vow."

"You'll only slow my efforts to save the princesses."

I picked up my skirts and ran faster. The bottles of milk clinked within the blankets, and I hoped they wouldn't break. I'd asked the wet nurse to accompany me, but she'd been too fearful to even think of trying to sneak out, especially when I'd revealed my hastily devised plan to jump from one of the rear castle windows into the moat and swim, pushing the two satchels ahead of me in the water. It didn't matter that the moat was filled with refuse or that the enemy surrounded the banks. I was counting on the cover of darkness to conceal me.

Did this knight have another, better plan? Perhaps he could be of some use to me.

"Where are you intending to take the princesses?" I called after him.

"It's best if you don't know, my lady," he retorted. "Then you won't have to worry about Ethelwulf torturing the information out of you."

Torture? I shuddered.

The knight and his companion entered the stairwell

of one of the many castle towers. I wasn't far behind, my footsteps slapping against the stone stairs, my breath starting to come in heavy bursts from my exertion. I grew almost dizzy from the speed of our descent, the rapid winding in the narrow stairwell.

Without warning, the knights halted at a landing before a closed door. I rushed down the last few steps between us, finally catching up. "I must insist—"

My statement was cut off by the door flying open and someone hurtling into the stairwell with a screech that sent chills racing up my spine. The first knight was holding both satchels in the same hand and had unsheathed his sword in the other. He swung his weapon through the air with such strength and speed that I heard it swoosh and then slice.

At the same moment, the second, taller knight threw his dagger so that it flew end over end, the silver blade flashing its deadly sharpness. I didn't understand why he'd tossed his knife until another screaming blur launched into the stairwell. The knife hit the intruder directly in the heart, the speed and force of the motion sending the blade deep and killing the attacker on impact.

Through the light emanating from the wall sconces placed strategically on either side of the door, I could only stare at the carnage, my mind trying to make sense of what I was seeing. One of the dead had black hair that hung in tangled locks, half hiding a crinkled leathery face that resembled a shriveled prune, parched lips still open in a dying scream. The dark skin was strange, something I'd never seen before and had only heard in tales.

When the shorter knight glanced at me, I realized

my face was likely a frozen mask of terror.

"Saracens," he said in a hard voice. "You should have heeded me and stayed in the queen's chambers."

I lifted my chin. "If I carry the satchels, you will have your hands free to better protect the princesses."

The knight's keen eyes flickered with surprise before both his mouth and jaw hardened.

"She's right, Lance," the taller knight said. "I suspect she'll help more than you think."

Lance. I tested the knight's given name, repeating it silently and studying him. Underneath the grime and grizzle lay a face with sturdy, chiseled features that some women might have considered handsome.

He seemed to be weighing my suggestion seriously. For a fraction of a second. Then he thrust the satchels at me. "Stay right behind me."

I didn't wait for another invitation. Stuffing my bundle of blankets and bottles inside, I peeked to see that both the babes were now asleep before sealing the bags properly. Then I hefted the satchels onto my arms at my elbows.

The weight of each with the babes, bottles, and blankets was heavier than I'd anticipated, but I was determined to do my part in saving the princesses. If this young knight could lead me to safety outside the castle, from there I'd surely be able to find a way to Everly and the Princess Constance before King Ethelwulf learned where she was and sent his soldiers to capture her.

Lance had already resumed his rapid descent. His friend waited more patiently for me as I started down once more. I hurried to catch up with Lance, stumbling over the hem of my gown while the other knight followed behind me.

When we reached the bottom, the dampness made me realize we were underground. Lance paused in front of a door and listened. Then, with a flick and twist of his knife, he picked the lock, threw it aside, and swung open the door, revealing a storage room filled with crates, barrels, and miscellaneous items of furniture and decorations.

We were obviously in the wrong place. But the thought of climbing back up the stairs made me sag against the wall, my arms already aching from the bags. My previous plans had included walking until daylight, at which point I'd hoped to find a ride in the wagon of anyone else fleeing from Delsworth. But with the weight of the bags, perhaps I wouldn't be able to walk as far as I'd hoped.

The tall knight retrieved a torch from the wall sconce outside the door. He lifted it, shining light into the room while Lance scanned the contents. He focused on something on the opposite wall and crossed over, shoving boxes and barrels aside.

"It's here," he said, scraping at a stone.

"Good." The tall knight held the light higher so that it illuminated the wall.

"We have no time to look for jewels or other valuables to take with us," I stated, but then stopped as suspicion took root. What if they were attempting to steal from the king for their own personal profit?

Before I could voice my mistrust, Lance dug away the mortar between the stones to reveal a deep groove. He stuck his gloved fingers into the slit and then pulled until he strained with the effort.

Stone scraped upon stone. To my astonishment, a

section of the wall began to slide open like a door, screeching louder and echoing past us up into the tower stairwell that we had just descended. Lance stopped and met the gaze of his comrade. Something somber passed between them.

"Take my knife." Lance tossed it, and the other knight caught it easily as if they made a practice of throwing knives as young boys did balls.

"You'll need it."

"You'll need it more." At the echo of a faint scream from somewhere in the stairwell, Lance motioned to me. "Let's go."

He didn't have to say anything else. I already knew what that screech meant. There were more Saracens inside the castle. It wouldn't take long for the enemy to hear the news of the birth of the twins—if they hadn't already—and then they'd be desperate to find us and prevent our escape.

The question was how many more Saracens were there? And would we be able to fend them all off?

My skin crawled at the thought of facing such quick warriors. Whom was I fooling? I wouldn't be able to fend off a single Saracen, much less a whole horde of them.

Urgency prodded me forward, and I ducked through the opening in the stone wall.

"Watch your step," Lance cautioned.

At the sight of another staircase—this one descending straight down—I pressed against the wall. With a torch in one hand, Lance stepped halfway through then stopped. He cast one more glance at his companion, who stood in the doorway.

"God be with you, Baldric." He fisted his hand to

his heart and thumped it twice.

Baldric repeated the motion. "God go with you too, my friend."

Another screech, this one nearer, drifted on the dank air. The door scraped as Baldric closed it from the other side.

Lance reached for one of the satchels. I released it to his strong grip. Just as I started to heft the second bag up on my arm again, he snagged it.

"I shall carry it." I tried tugging it back. He didn't relinquish his grasp. "You lead the way with the torch. And I'll carry the princesses."

I wanted to protest, but his glance at the stone door silenced me. Actually, the sadness in his eyes cut off my words, for I realized then what the two knights had already known. Baldric would hold off the Saracens for as long as possible, but he'd eventually die in his efforts to give us a head start out of the castle.

I let Lance take both bags. Then, with the torch in hand, I started my descent into endless darkness.

"Faster," Lance said from behind me.

Without a railing, I braced myself against the wall, which was damp and slimy. I tried to pick up my pace, wanting to prove Lance hadn't made a mistake in helping me with the princesses. But I suspected he could travel at double my speed and I was slowing down his escape. Perhaps I should have allowed him to proceed without me. Had I been foolish to insist on accompanying him, and would I cost the princesses their lives?

By the time we reached the bottom of the stairs, I was breathless again. I thrust the light out so we could see down the tunnel ahead. Supported overhead with wooden beams, the passageway easily allowed me to stand straight, but it wasn't tall enough for a man of Lance's build. I hesitated at the sight of the writhing tangles dangling from the ceiling. Roots? Water?

"Are we under the moat?" I asked, creeping tentatively forward.

"Aye."

I swallowed a breath of panic at the thought of being underneath the body of water that surrounded the castle. My mind conjured pictures of the tunnel walls caving in and water pouring over us. I'd much rather be swimming in the moat than drowning underneath it. But now that I was here, I had no choice but to advance.

I ducked under the first roots even as they slithered and twisted as though alive.

"Down!" Lance shouted.

I dropped at the same moment one of his hands pressed against my head, forcing me to the side. A second later, he slashed his sword into the roots. A hissing mass hit the floor by my feet, where the torchlight illuminated the pile. I found myself staring at over a dozen pairs of beady black eyes and bared fangs.

These were no roots. They were severed snake bodies.

With a scream, I released the torch and scrambled back, desperate to get away from the writhing heap. Their snapping and hissing faded. Even so, I trembled with terror at the realization I'd almost walked into the serpents.

Lance retrieved the torch and held it out to me. "We have to keep going."

"No. I cannot." Ahead, more clusters of snakes writhed together in clumps, and some slid out of holes in the ceiling as if they'd heard my screams and had come to join in feasting upon my blood.

Before I could protest again, Lance thrust the satchels into my hands, giving me no choice but to cling to the princesses. He started forward, swinging his sword back and forth like a farmer with his scythe at harvest. Snakes fell to the floor and thrashed for a few seconds before lying still. He shoved the bloody bodies aside and motioned for me to follow him.

I swallowed hard, wanting to retreat but realizing I had no other way out of the castle, that if I'd jumped into the moat as I'd planned, I likely would have been attacked and killed by the serpents that apparently made the land surrounding the castle their home.

Lance moved quickly, chopping a path, killing without hesitation. I scurried after him, dodging the carcasses even as they released their dying hisses and stared at me with their ebony eyes. If he could exude such courage, I had to as well.

We hiked much farther than I expected before the snakes finally began to thin and then stop altogether. The path steepened and turned rocky. My arms ached under the load of the bags, and I stumbled over a sharp stone.

As though Lance had been keeping one eye upon me, he pivoted and steadied me, before peering back through the darkness. His lips pursed together in displeasure. "We must go faster," he said tersely as he relieved me of one of the satchels.

"You set the pace, and I shall endeavor to stay with you." Again, I wanted to prove he hadn't made a mistake in bringing me along.

He said no more, but lengthened his stride, climbing with a nimbleness of a hare and making my efforts look all the clumsier in comparison. Even so, I strained to remain close behind him, determined not to lag even when my lungs burned, my sides cramped, and my legs trembled with the exertion.

I was relieved when the tunnel narrowed, forcing us to slow down and crawl on our hands and knees. As we pushed the satchels along, I calmed my breathing and steadied my shaking limbs.

When we finally arrived at a ledge that opened into a cave, Lance lowered himself first, dropping easily to the dirt floor. He held out the torch, revealing a small cavern that seemed harmless enough.

After he secured the torch, I handed him first one satchel then the other. I dangled my legs off the ledge, intending to lower myself the way he had. But before I could gather the courage to jump, he reached for me, fitting his hands at my hips and effortlessly lifting me. For an instant, as I was suspended, I could feel the power of his arms and upper body. I had seen the king's guard always from a distance and had known they were the fiercest, fittest, and fastest men in the land. But I hadn't understood the reality of their position and strength until now.

He lowered me to the ground as carefully as he had the princesses but released me without a second glance. I might be awed by his prowess in aiding our escape, but he clearly was not enamored with me.

"Where do we go from here?" I took stock of the cave, which was riddled with cobwebs and dust as though no one but spiders had been in it for decades.

"We find the exit." He crossed to the opposite wall. There he kicked at a lump and caused dust to plume into the air. He rolled the lump over to reveal a leather shoulder bag.

"See if there's anything in the supply bag we can use," he instructed as he moved to the wall and began tapping it with the hilt of his sword.

I knelt next to the bag and brushed away the dust. Gingerly I lifted the flap, and a hemp rope fell out. Before I could dig deeper, Lance was already shifting aside an enormous stone, leaning into it with his shoulder. He strained, his muscles bulging as the scraping rock gave way to crumbling pebbles and an opening. Mist sprayed into the room, bringing the scent of wet rocks and soil. Along with it came the rushing sound of water.

At the same moment, the distant shout of voices wafted from the tunnel hole behind us. I shivered and stood. The Saracens had made it past Lance's comrade. I had no idea how much time we had before they'd be upon us, but I suspected it wasn't long.

Slinging the dusty pack over my shoulder, I picked up both satchels and carried them to the cave exit where Lance peered out. I wasn't sure what he could see through the darkness of the night, but when he spun to face me, his expression was etched with determination. He grabbed the rope from where I'd left it and began to rapidly uncoil it and hand me one end. "Tie this around your waist."

As shouts echoed in the tunnel, I hurried to do his bidding, but my fingers fumbled over one another in my haste.

"After I leap," he said brushing aside my fingers and

cinching the rope for me, "I want you to jump with the princesses. Hang onto the bags and don't let them go."

Jump? I couldn't squeeze a response past my constricting throat.

He hesitated, glancing at one of the bags. Then he lifted his gaze to mine. "You'll be fine."

I could only nod mutely. In the flickering from the torch, his eyes were dark and brooding and yet somehow comforting.

"I'll be waiting for you." His voice was calm, almost soothing. "I'll have the other end of the rope and will use it to find you and the princesses."

I nodded again.

He took the pack from my shoulder, strapped it on his, and then moved to the cave entrance, where he climbed outside and stood on a narrow ledge, the rope tied to his waist. "Once I disappear," he called over the roaring, "count to ten before following me."

Only then did I notice the rapidly flowing water pouring down over the ledge and forming a wall in front of him. A waterfall. We'd come out of the tunnel at the backside of a waterfall. For a second, I stared at the cascading silver sheet and spraying diamond drops. The waterfall was magnificent even from the back.

"Throw the torch in after me," he commanded. Then he spun and launched himself into the air.

I gasped as the water swallowed and carried him away, its steady crashing reminding me I would have to do the very same thing next. The realization paralyzed me. I had no idea what was at the bottom. What if I fell and hit rocks? What if I drowned? What if I let go of one of the babes?

Panic threatened to propel me back. But at shouts

that were much too close, I realized I had no choice but to jump. I crawled out onto the ledge and stood. My legs shook, as did my hands. I situated the bags one on each arm, made sure they were securely sealed, and then tossed the torch into the rushing water.

Immediately darkness surrounded me. I hadn't counted to ten as Lance had asked, and I didn't know if ten seconds had passed or ten minutes. But at an urgent call from the cave behind me, I knew I'd run out of time.

I closed my eyes, whispered a silent prayer, and then jumped.

Chapter 4

LANCE

THE ROPE PULLED TAUT AGAINST MY WAIST. HAND OVER HAND I wound the hemp, struggling to pull it as fast as I could. I prayed the young noblewoman had been able to keep hold of the princesses during the drop. Although it wasn't more than two dozen feet, the impact would strain her.

As I wrestled to drag the weight of the woman to myself, I had to admit even if she had been more of a burden than help during the escape from the castle, I didn't know how I would have carried the princesses through the tunnel and simultaneously slashed away the dangerous snakes. And though I could have jumped the waterfall with the princesses, the current was swift just as I'd expected, and I would have had a difficult time locating and swimming to a safe alcove while holding on to the bags. As it was, I'd found a place near the middle of the river underneath a thick pile of branches that had formed a small dam against several large boulders.

At the brush of a hand, I drew her close. "I've got you," I assured as she groped for me. The force of the water slammed her into my body, and I wound my arm around her waist at the same time that she clung to my chest. Both princess bags floated on either side of her and had apparently acted as buoys to keep her above water. Even so, she coughed and spluttered, likely having swallowed water during the jump.

"The princesses?" she asked through her coughing.

I unfastened the bags enough to stick my hand inside. Though the interiors were slightly damp, the well-cushioned infants were still asleep from what I could tell.

"They're fine," I said, closing the bags tightly.

Alert to danger, I glanced around, attempting to assess our location. A thick mantle of clouds covered the dark night sky, giving us additional shelter. Even so, the Saracens had an uncanny tracking ability and might be able to see us if we weren't extremely careful.

I kicked my feet to stay afloat, relieved I'd looped my belt around one of the larger branches to prevent us from being swept away in the rapidly moving river. The young noblewoman leaned her head against my shoulder and coughed again. Her entire body trembled, and I tightened my hold, although I didn't know why. Perhaps to reassure her?

Grudgingly I had to give her praise. I didn't know of any woman—noble or not—who would have dared to jump into the unknown with such unquestioning obedience the way she had.

Heretofore, I hadn't known much about women except what I'd witnessed from afar. As a member of the king's guard, I'd vowed to give the king the best years of my youth. I'd had no time or opportunity for meeting women. Even if I had, the elite guards pledged celibacy until we were discharged by old age or death.

Most, like me, expected to serve until death, and I'd been more than willing to make such a sacrifice. After all, very few tradesmen's sons had the opportunity to train to be a knight. That was reserved for nobility. But because of my exceptional physical abilities, my father had made sure I was noticed by the lord who owned the Stefford smelter he worked at. Father hadn't wanted me to end up toiling long hours in so dangerous a place. He'd wanted more for me, for all of his family.

I'd been devastated when he'd died several years ago when I'd still been a squire. If only he'd lived to see how far I'd risen in the ranks of the king's elite guards. I consoled myself that even though he was no longer there to support my mother, two sisters, and two brothers, I earned enough for them to live comfortably.

The young noblewoman didn't lift her head from my shoulder. Her breath came in gasps, her exhaustion and fear evident in each exhale. I'd never been so near to a woman, never even touched one except as a means of protection.

Now I was suddenly keenly aware of the way her legs intertwined with mine, the pressure of her body, and the warmth of her breathing against my neck. I couldn't keep from remembering how exquisitely beautiful she was— the long, smooth line of her neck, the curved elegance of her chin and jaw. And her eyes. They were such a mesmerizing shade of green, a man might lose himself there.

Not me. I'd never succumbed to a woman's charm. I'd vowed not to let my manly desires awaken. Had vowed to keep that part of myself shut away. And I wouldn't start now.

As though sensing the direction of my thoughts and

our awkward entanglement, the young noblewoman started to push away from me.

I didn't release her, not because I wanted her near, but because our very lives depended upon our stillness. "We must hide until they are gone."

"Do you think they will find us?" she asked close to my ear so I would hear her above the rushing river and waterfall.

"They are excellent trackers, but they don't like water and won't come into the river to look for us. More likely, they'll camp out on the banks and wait for us to emerge."

She was quiet for a moment, absorbing my words. "So, you are hoping they will search for us down-river?"

"Aye."

"And when they are gone, we shall make our escape?"

"Aye."

"At least the water is not overly cold."

The chill of the river hadn't crossed my mind. I'd been in much colder water during my days in training. I suppose if I had to watch over this woman in addition to the princesses, the mild midsummer temperatures would make my job easier.

Her long, wet hair swirled around her on the water, brushing against my arm. As she clung tightly to the bags, she had no free hands for tucking her wet strands away, and I was surprised by my desire to gather her locks and comb them together.

"You have not asked my name," she said, her mouth still close to my ear.

"Nor you mine." Although I wanted to ask when such introductions should have been possible—perhaps in between slaying Saracens or while frantically chopping snakes in half or maybe before I'd jumped into the waterfall?

As it was, we had only minutes until the Saracens swarmed the riverbanks. Our introductions had to be quick.

"You are Lance. I heard your companion say it. And I am Lady Felicia of Avington."

I searched my mind for any recognition of the name but could find nothing.

"My father, Lord Avington, is one of the king's advisors," she offered.

"Did he evacuate with the others?"

She shook her head. "No." Her voice dropped so that I could barely hear it above the river. "He stayed because he did not want to leave me behind."

My thoughts returned to the noblemen who had remained with the king, those who had been in his chamber with him when he'd died.

"What will happen to him?" she asked, the nearness of her breath making my neck tingle. "To all those in the castle?"

"I don't know." I closed my eyes for a second, wanting to believe Ethelwulf would allow them to live. The rules of warfare stated the terms of surrender: those of the nobility who bowed their knee to the new lord and pledged their allegiance should be spared their lives. I prayed Ethelwulf would honor that rule, although I suspected he was operating by his own standards. And I had no doubt many would be too loyal to King Francis to submit.

My eyes flew open as my instincts told me the Saracens had found a way out of the cave that didn't involve jumping from the waterfall. They'd likely climbed down the rocky cliff instead. And now they were close by on both riverbanks.

Pushing out of hiding, I scanned the river's edges and saw what I'd dreaded. The flicker of torches. Quickly, I floated back into the covering of branches, drawing us into the tangle of debris as far as I could.

Felicia started to speak again, but I bent in and pressed my mouth into her ear. "They're near."

She froze.

For long moments, I didn't move either, relishing the gentle curves, smooth skin, and the warmth against my lips. An inner warning reminded me to distance myself, to keep a wall between us, to remain the detached warrior. Doing anything less could compromise the mission, distract me, dull my keen senses.

Nevertheless, a slow heat began to burn in my gut, a strange sensation I'd never experienced before. The heat spread until every nerve in my body was entirely too aware of her and the fact she was a woman. I couldn't seem to stop the warmth from seeping outward to my limbs. Nor did I want to. Rather I wanted to press closer and breathe deeply of her. And only with the greatest of willpower did I hold myself back.

Was this what had happened to my few comrades who'd been dismissed from the guard? Had they been unable to resist the pull, the sway, of a beautiful woman?

Don't let the feelings start, I mentally chided. *Keep the door entirely closed.* One crack could ruin the self-made control I'd developed into an iron will.

When she finally shifted slightly, I released a tense breath, but just as quickly sucked it in when she moved in closer, letting her forehead brush my jaw, her warm breath even nearer to my neck. She relaxed as if resting in the arms of a man was a perfectly normal, everyday occurrence for her. Perhaps it was. After all, she was a courtier at the royal residence not only to serve the queen but also to find a husband.

And had she? She likely had many men vying for her hand in marriage. No doubt she would be a favorite among the court. How could she not be? I hadn't known her long, but even in the short time I'd been with her, I'd seen her courage and determination and dedication.

A shout from the bank forced my attention to the danger of the present circumstances. At the reflection of torchlight over the water, I ducked lower in the water, praying the glimmer wouldn't reach and expose us. If it came near, we would have to completely submerge for a few seconds.

As the light drifted closer, I held my breath. Thankfully, Felicia seemed to do the same, sensing the growing danger.

When the light moved away, I let the tension ease from my shoulders. Even then, I remained silent, knowing the enemy still might be on the shore attempting to deceive us into thinking they were gone.

My mind spun with a dozen strategies for a dozen situations in which we might find ourselves. I had to be prepared for anything. Primarily I needed to decide where to hide the princesses once we were free from the Saracens. I wanted to stay in the river so that the skilled warriors wouldn't be able to trace our scent or track our trail. But they'd be expecting such a move and would fan out further downriver and wait for our appearance. We'd have to go overland.

I conjured images of the detailed maps I'd had to memorize. I'd had to learn every valley and hill along with every creek and brook in the land. Now I understood why. For long minutes, I plotted our possible escape routes, discarding one for another. I tried to determine how quickly we could go and how far we could get before the babies would awaken and need attention.

If I could keep my thoughts focused on strategy, I could keep them off Felicia. The moment I stopped planning, my mind had a will of its own and came back to her, to her warm breath, which had grown soft and even against my neck.

After a short while, my instincts and the silence on the riverbanks told me the Saracens had moved on. It was time to make our escape.

"My lady," I whispered.

She didn't respond.

"We must go now."

"Hmmm," came her answer.

Had she fallen asleep? I calculated the passing of the hours since I'd first heard rumors the queen had been in labor. When was the last time this young woman had slept? Two days ago?

I was accustomed to staying awake for days, had been trained to work with sleep deprivation. But how fast and long would this noblewoman be able to run without rest?

Frustration cascaded into my veins. I should have insisted she remain in the castle with the others. How would we stay ahead of our pursuers if she began to tire?

"My lady," I said louder. "Time to leave."

She nestled against me, her nose grazing my neck where the mantle of my chain mail left it exposed. I swallowed hard and gathered the inner reserves of my will together. Then I gently pried her loose.

I sensed her wakefulness even before she yawned.

"Hold onto the bags," I instructed. "I'll lead the way to the opposite bank."

As I began to move, once more she obeyed me without question. Tugging her behind me, I fought the current and attempted to stay a straight course, my muscles straining with each rapid stroke. When we reached the riverbank, I placed my hand upon her arm to communicate the need to remain silent. With the satchels on the ground in front of her, she checked on the princesses as I crept forward and surveyed the area.

When I was positive we were alone, I led her up the bank and into the woodland, then returned to the river to do the best I could to erase our tracks. Once I was sure we'd left no trace of our presence there, I took one of the satchels from Felicia.

"The babes are damp but still asleep," she whispered as she stood. She'd been wise to choose bags covered in pig bladder to make them waterproof.

In the darkness of the thick woodland, I could see only the faintest outline of her. "We need to run if we have any hope of distancing ourselves from anyone who might follow us."

"I can run," she said, although somewhat tremulously.

"Your skirts will hinder your movement." My face heated with embarrassment at the mention of her attire. Again, I had no experience with women's garments and had no wish for any impropriety. But the urgency of the situation overruled all else.

"I shall tie them up," she said. "With the rope."

I handed her my belt instead. "Use this, my lady."

She worked rapidly to roll up the long folds of her dress. When she was finished, I was glad for the cover of darkness that hid her. Even so, I hiked forward rapidly lest I happen to see her. The crackling of sticks and brush told me she was following. And I prayed we would be safe despite her noise.

"Stay close," I said over my shoulder as I began to run. The pace was not as fast or vigorous as I was accustomed to. Nevertheless, I could sense her struggling to keep up, stumbling over windfalls and slipping on leaves. Her breath came in gasps, and she inhaled sharply at the slap of a twig or the snag of a bramble. Otherwise, she kept going without complaint.

After we'd been running for some time, I expected her to ask for a respite, but she didn't speak—a fact for which I was grateful. My mind was carving a mental path through the woodland, and the fewer distractions, the better I'd be able to focus. Without the moon and with only a few stars to guide me, I was relying mostly upon my memorization of Mercia's maps to lead me to the Cress River.

Once we reached the waterway, I'd use a few of the silver pieces inside the pack I'd found in the cave to rent a small boat. Then I'd row as quickly upriver as I could. The Cress would eventually split into three branches—the Upper, Central, and Lower. From there, I'd pray Ethelwulf wouldn't be able to figure out which direction we took.

But if our pursuers were able to track us, I didn't know how we could outrun them forever.

Chapter
5

Felicia

I awoke with a start, my eyes flying open to find the fog that had shrouded the boat earlier had lifted to reveal low clouds with dark, angry bellies. A tiny wail came from one of the bags next to me, and I realized the babes were hungry again.

I sat forward and had to bite back a groan. Every muscle and bone ached from the endless run through the woodland of the previous night. I'd wanted to stop on countless occasions, had thought I'd die from exhaustion. But every time I considered resting, I remembered my vow to the queen. She'd trusted me with the task of saving her babes. I had to remain strong for her and for the princesses.

When Lance had finally halted, I'd collapsed into a heap on the ground, my entire body trembling. I'd known once I was down I wouldn't be able to rise again. I'd despaired that he might have to leave me behind—until he returned from a short excursion to inform me he'd rented a boat. At the news, I'd nearly wept with relief.

After he'd assisted me into the small skiff, I'd dropped to the hull, wanting nothing more than to close my eyes in exhaustion. But the herbal sleeping medicine given to the babes had finally worn off, and they'd chosen that moment to awaken. I'd had to search deep within myself for the stamina to feed and change them. Thankfully, they'd fallen asleep again without fussing. I'd tucked them securely into the bags and then succumbed to my fatigue.

How long had I slept?

Lance sat at the middle bench only a couple feet away plunging the oars in and out of the water with the same deep and swift rhythm he'd used during the dark hours of the morning. Hadn't he stopped once in all the time I'd slept? His attention was as keenly alert to our surroundings as it had been from the moment we'd started the journey, his gaze constantly shifting from the distant riverbanks to the other boats sharing the watercourse with us.

After I'd insisted on the Upper Cress River as our route of escape rather than the other branches, he'd relented, for which I was grateful. The upper branch led to Everly, where the rest of the king's courtiers, along with Princess Constance, had gone after evacuating Delsworth.

As a major waterway on the Great Isle, the Cress River was always busy with barges from the coast transporting goods up to the Iron Cities as well as boats bringing iron bars created in smelters downriver to the port, where they were shipped to other nations.

Today the tributary was busy, the waterfronts hectic and crowded, boats loaded down with people and belongings. I guessed word had already spread about the royal couple's death and the capital city falling to King Ethelwulf, and now anyone who could leave and go into hiding was doing so.

Another cry like that of a kitten's mew drew me to my knees. I unbuckled the flap on the first bag to find that Princess Emmeline was awake. She peered up at me, her eyes wide and curious. One of her hands had come loose from her swaddling, and she reached it out as if to greet me.

I couldn't help but give the wee one a smile. Even though her face was ruddy and wrinkled, her features were delicate and adorable and her hair a fuzzy dark brown. I touched the soft baby flesh of her hand and was surprised when her fingers closed around my thumb in a tight grip.

Adjusting my hold, I lifted her out as gently as I could and situated her in my arms, all the while letting the babe hold my finger. Her serious eyes seemed to search my face as though to wonder who I was and why I'd taken the place of her mother.

At the thought of the queen's beautiful but lifeless body, hot tears pricked my eyes, and I placed a kiss on the poor motherless babe's cheek. When I glanced up, I caught Lance watching me. He looked quickly away, but not before I saw approval in his expression that warmed me. After trying hard not to be a burden to him last night, I'd felt like a failure at every move. Was it possible he didn't resent my presence so much after all?

I dug out one of the bottles from the bottom of the satchel and began feeding Emmeline. As I did so, I took the opportunity to study Lance more carefully. We'd been so rushed and the night so dark that I hadn't really taken him in.

He'd discarded his mantle of chain mail and now wore a peasant-like cloak and hood that he'd acquired at some point—likely to conceal himself from recognition as one of the king's elite guards. Even with his head covered, I glimpsed his blond hair with hints of brown. As was customary for trained soldiers, his locks were braided back on his scalp in three plaits that were tied together at the base of his neck. The style lent him a fierceness that was accentuated by the thick muscles of his shoulders and arms and chest.

The time in the river after jumping from the waterfall had washed away the battle blood that had covered him. While his countenance was grimy from the miles we'd traversed through the forest and now the hours he'd spent rowing, his features were clear in the daylight—a prominent brow above dark-brown eyes that seemed to see everyone and everything, a wide square jaw, a defined dimple in the cleft of his chin, a determined mouth, and a surprisingly straight nose. As before when I'd first met him, I was struck by his rugged handsomeness.

He was also certainly impressive with his strength and his endurance. Surely, he was as tired as I by now and could use a respite from rowing.

"Would you like me to relieve you for a while?" I asked, breaking the silence between us.

"Nay." He slid me another sideways look, darting a glance at my legs.

Only then did I realize I hadn't yet untucked my skirt from under his belt. Mortified that my ankles were exposed so brazenly, even if my stockings covered them, I loosened my skirt and pulled it down. "Do you believe we are safe now?" I asked, smoothing the layers and trying to sound more composed than I felt.

"Once Ethelwulf realizes the royal princesses have escaped the castle, he won't rest until he captures them." Lance studied one passing skiff after another as though assessing each one for danger.

I swallowed my fear and watched Emmeline suckle the bottle for a moment, her lids growing heavy. "I— we must find a safe place for the princesses."

"I'm planning to take them to St. Cuthbert's, an abbey hidden in the far eastern part of the Iron Hills."

I noticed how he didn't include me in his plans. "If it is hidden, how then shall we find it?"

"Have no doubt. I'll find it."

I bristled at his arrogance. "We must retrieve the Princess Constance in Everly first. I promised the queen I would protect the child."

He pursed his lips and started to shake his head.

"We shall pass near the city on our way to the Iron Hills," I continued. "We must take Princess Constance away to safety before King Ethelwulf sends his mercenaries to kill her."

"If I delay any further, I'll risk the lives of the new-born babes."

"She is the heir to the throne," I insisted.

Lance rowed steadily, meeting my gaze hesitantly. I could sense his desire to uphold the formality between us due to our stations. He clearly lived by a high code of honor and wanted to maintain his integrity. But because of the unusual circumstances, he was over-stepping the usual boundaries and he knew it. "If I go into Everly, I could very well be walking into a trap."

"I shall go in by myself. No one will suspect that a young woman like me would attempt to steal the princess away. I shall find her and then meet you outside the city." The idea of venturing off by myself terrified me, especially after seeing Saracens. But I couldn't allow Lance to sense my fear or he'd never agree to get Princess Constance.

When he seemed to consider my option seriously, I let my body loosen with relief. But a moment later, he shook his head. "Nay. 'Tis too dangerous."

"I shall take great care."

"You'll stand out." His eyes flickered down the length of my once elegant gown, now snagged and damp and dirty.

"I shall find a clean gown—"

"You'll stand out for who you are, not for what you wear."

"Then I shall disguise myself."

"And how will you disguise your beauty?" The moment he said the words, he looked away and clamped his jaw, embarrassment rippling across his features.

My beauty. Usually, I gained no pleasure from references to my appearance. Flattery at court was too commonplace and the focus on outward features too important. But I suspected Lance was not one to notice or remark on a woman's comeliness often, if at all. Somehow the rarity of his praise made it more valuable.

I took in his poor cloak. "We shall dress as peasants."

"If you're dressed as a peasant, how will you gain

access to the castle and the princess?"

"My brother Charles and his betrothed live in Everly. I shall ask to see him."

Lance didn't immediately reject my proposal, and I took hope from that.

"We could trade the boat for a farmer's wagon and garments," I continued. "And we could also pretend we are married, that the princesses are our babes."

"The news of the royal twins' birth will soon travel through the land."

"Then we shall only have one babe out at a time."

"And the Princess Constance? How will we explain her presence?"

"We shall tell her as much of the truth as she can understand." The bright young princess had been a joy and a delight to the queen and all the ladies-in-waiting. "She will cooperate and pretend we are her parents." At least I prayed she would.

Lance was silent for a moment, lifting the oars and then dipping them back into the water as effortlessly as if he'd been born for the task. His arms strained underneath the cloak, and the muscles in his neck rippled once again showing his strength and reminding me how much I needed him if I hoped to succeed in keeping my vow to the queen.

"Very well," he finally said, although somewhat testily. "We'll go to Everly first."

The sourness of sweat permeated the tunic Lance had purchased for me when we'd docked along the busy quay of Everly. I attempted to ignore the stench as I made my way along the city's main thoroughfare. The coarse brown wool chafed my legs, and the simple leather boots I'd also acquired clomped against the cobbled street, especially since they were too big for my petite feet. I'd covered my hair with a rectangular veil tied in place with a cord that wound around my forehead. The veil didn't obscure my face, and so I ducked my head as I plodded along, attempting to keep my features as concealed as possible.

Like all the other towns we'd passed, word had already reached Everly of the king and queen's deaths. The usual smoke rising from the chimneys of the city's many iron smelters was noticeably absent even if the scent of the burning metal still hung heavy in the haze of eventide. Around me was bedlam, a mass exodus of people from the city so frenzied I could hardly push my way through the crowded streets.

Most were nobility fleeing to estates in the countryside, likely fearing to remain visible if King Ethelwulf should send his army farther inland. Others were peasant farmers selling their wares, concluding that they too would vacate to the country where perhaps they could avoid any confrontation with the new king of Mercia.

Surely by now King Ethelwulf had entered the castle at Delsworth and laid claim to the throne. If the rumors regarding his rule of Warwick were true, then nobleman and peasant alike had every right to be concerned.

The peaceful existence we'd known for more than a century, beginning long ago with the reign of King Alfred the Peacemaker, had come to an end. All the more reason to whisk Princess Constance to safety. King Ethelwulf wouldn't want to leave any rivals to the throne.

I hurried along in the direction of the castle gate, keeping my face averted so no one would see my fair, unblemished skin and beauty and realize I wasn't a peasant. I tried not to think about the difficulty of the task ahead, the fact that I needed to get inside the royal residence, locate the princess, change her into the plain child's garments we'd bought, and then attempt to walk back out of town to the eastern gate where Lance had said he'd wait. I had to do it without anyone suspecting who we were or what we were doing.

In addition, I had only two hours to accomplish it all. Before the sun descended and the city gate closed for the night. Even then, I couldn't keep from wondering if Lance would wait for me, that perhaps he was relieved to be rid of me so he could proceed without me slowing him down.

As I wound my way up the busy street that led to the castle gatehouse, I rehearsed my plan for getting inside. I would reveal myself to the guards, pray they would believe I was nobility, and then pay them each a silver coin from our few that remained.

Then I would request an audience with my brother Charles and hope he hadn't yet left the city. Among those fleeing, I'd already glimpsed many of the men and women from court, those who had evacuated Delsworth a few weeks ago. Yet I hadn't seen Charles or his betrothed among them. Nor had I seen the Princess Constance.

I glanced up toward the imposing fortress ahead. Built with a dozen stone towers and spires of varying shapes and sizes, the Everly royal residence was one of the most beautiful works of architecture in Mercia. Set on the high ground overlooking the Upper Cress River, it was more imposing than any other castle I'd seen.

I'd visited the palace last year when the court had traveled with the king and queen to Everly for the summer months. Since the city was within the shadows of the Iron Hills, it was cooler and less humid than the seaport capital of Delsworth.

I was vaguely familiar with the layout of the castle. Even so, it was enormous, and I couldn't waste precious time racing up and down its many spiraling staircases. Perhaps Charles would be able to lead me to the nursery and the princess more directly.

My foot snagged on a crack in the cobblestone and jolted me with the realization that if I consulted with Charles, I might put my entire family into jeopardy. If King Ethelwulf ever discovered I had anything to do with the escape of the princesses, he'd punish my relatives, likely torturing and killing them in an effort to locate me.

Already I'd endangered them. Most of the ladies, including the wet nurse, knew I was running away with the princesses. King Ethelwulf even now might be hunting me down. What if he'd already infiltrated the Everly royal residence with his spies? Or maybe Saracens were there waiting for me?

I stifled a shudder and forced my feet to keep moving. The simple truth was that if I wanted to help Princess Constance and fulfill my vow to the queen, I'd have to do it through my own ingenuity, without help from Charles or any other nobility who remained.

By the time I came upon the gatehouse, I'd decided

my only course was to try the lower servants' entrance and pay off the guards there. But Providence intervened with the timely arrival of a mule-drawn cart that bounced through the gatehouse followed by a large group of servants and nobility on foot. I broke away from the wall and used their activity as cover. Garnering only a few glances, I slid past them until I was inside the gatehouse. My legs and stomach quivered, and I expected a guard would bolt after me and demand to know my business.

But when no one approached, I dashed into the bailey, attempting to move as though I belonged and was on some urgent errand for a lord or lady. With each step, I waited for a soldier's shout to impede me. Strangely, no one opposed me.

Even so, I dared not enter through the castle's main entrance. Instead, I found a side doorway that water carriers used when lugging buckets inside the castle from the well. As the door closed behind me, eerie darkness and stillness greeted me.

Was I too late? Had someone already taken the Princess Constance away?

I raced through the corridors, praying I wouldn't get lost in the maze of passageways. Everywhere I went, the hallways were silent and rooms deserted. My heart sank lower with the realization the courtiers were gone, likely taking the guards with them.

When I reached the nursery chambers, I burst through the doors and stopped short at the sight of a stout old woman standing in front of the hearth, a long knife in her hands.

"Don't take one step closer," she said, pointing the weapon at me. I recognized the aged plump face framed with a curly mop of gray hair. This was Dot, the princess's nursemaid. Although I hadn't interacted with her often as she kept mainly to the nursery, I'd seen her on occasion, always pleasant and kind. Now angry almost vicious lines creased her forehead and turned down her eyebrows and mouth.

I held up my hands in a motion of surrender. "I seek Princess Constance."

Dot thrust the knife forward menacingly. "If you try to take her, I'll slice you up, that I will."

Only then did I see the tiny figure behind the old woman, plastered to her skirt, her fingers clutching the linen, a pale face peeking out.

At the sight of the familiar delicate features with silky blond curls falling in ringlets to dainty shoulders, I knelt and bowed my head. "Your Royal Highness." My relief at finding the princess was so overwhelming I blinked back tears.

At rapid footsteps behind me, I rose, but not in time. The sharp point of a blade pricked through my garments into my spine. "You'd best be on your way, missy," came a younger woman's voice, followed by another painful jab into my skin.

My mind raced even as I kept my body motionless. What had I expected? To be able to walk into the nursery and carry Princess Constance off without anyone questioning me? Even if I explained to Dot who I was and even if she happened to remember me from among the many noblewomen who surrounded the queen, why would she give me the princess?

Lance had cautioned me, had told me I needed a better plan for getting through the castle, and I hadn't listened to him.

"Please." I attempted to keep the anxiety out of my voice. "The queen sent me to take Princess Constance to safety. I must be on my way before the city gates close."

The older woman scrutinized me, taking in my peasant attire. I wanted to remove my veil and fully identify myself, but I dared not budge with the knife biting my flesh. Instead, I tried to think of a new solution, a way to convince them both to hand the princess over.

"You are Dot, the princess's nursemaid," I said. "Why are you still here? Why are you not making efforts to leave like everyone else?"

At my knowledge of her name, surprise flickered through her eyes. "Who are you?"

"It is best for you not to know," I replied. "But I can tell you that I gave the queen my solemn word to come for Connie." I purposefully used the queen's nickname for the little girl.

Upon hearing her mother's pet name, the princess circled around the front of her nursemaid, her big blue eyes wide and full of questions. "Go to Mommy?" the little girl asked, stepping toward me.

Dot reached for Constance to stop her, but the princess slipped easily from her grasp. The nursemaid took a wobbling step after the girl, then halted and grimaced at the pain the movement caused her.

Her foot was wrapped in bandages, but from the oozing and swelling, I could see she was ailing from gout or perhaps an injury that wasn't healing. Though she might be able to take a step or two, she certainly couldn't manage the long passageways and numerous staircases. In her condition, she couldn't leave the castle, even if she wanted to flee with Princess Constance.

"Why have you not made arrangements for someone else to take the princess?" I asked. "With so many others departing, surely you could have found guards to protect her?"

Dot pulled herself up and glared at me. "I hid the princess while the others left, letting everyone believe she was gone."

"Why would you do such a thing?"

"Who can I trust? No telling which nobles might want to take the princess directly to King Ethelwulf in order to save themselves." Dot looked at me pointedly as if that's exactly why I was there.

"I have no intention of turning the princess over to King Ethelwulf."

"I tried to convince my daughter to take the princess and go on without me, that I did." Dot waved to the woman behind me who still pressed the blade into my back. "But she refuses to leave me here alone after we heard the news."

"What news?"

"A few hours ago, we received word that King Ethelwulf is sending a contingent of mercenaries north to Everly. They'll be here by nightfall."

A contingent was on its way? Already? I'd hoped for more time to make a safe getaway. Now a new sense of urgency burned through me. "No doubt the first place they will search is the royal residence and the nursery."

"I was planning to hide the princess again."

Lance had said the Saracens were excellent trackers, which meant the princess would be in danger anywhere in the palace or even in Everly. "There is no hiding place here safe enough, and I need to take her away now." I held out my hand to the little girl. "Come, Connie,"

The princess hesitated, looking between Dot and me.

"I shall take you to your new sisters." I spoke more to reassure Dot than Princess Constance.

"You have the babes?" the old nursemaid asked, a light finally starting to glow in her eyes. The pressure of the daughter's knife against my spine eased.

"The less you know," I replied, "the safer for us all." I refused to think what King Ethelwulf might do to this old woman once he learned she was connected to Princess Constance. He'd surely torture her to wrest every bit of information out of her regarding the princess's whereabouts.

"I'll die before I betray the princesses," Dot said in a wobbly voice, her eyes brimming with tears.

"Even so, I must say no more."

Resignation settled within the lines of her face. She had no other choice but to entrust the princess to me, and she knew it.

Dot and her daughter helped me ready the princess for the journey, changing her into the plain clothes I'd brought along, packing a bag of food and supplies as well as goat's milk for the babes. Finally, they said their good-byes to the princess. Thankfully, Princess Constance appeared to sense the gravity of the situation, obeying Dot's instructions to remain strong and brave.

"Keep this for the princess, my lady," Dot said once we were ready to go. She pressed something solid into my hand. It was a ring. And not just an ordinary ring. It was the king's signet ring containing the royal emblem of Mercia—two golden lions standing rampant, their paws touching the ruby at the center.

"King Francis sent it with the princess when she came to Everly," Dot explained. "Now you must take it and make sure it stays with her wherever God may lead her."

"I shall endeavor to do so," I said, sensing the importance of the ring—that perhaps the princess would one day need it to prove she was the heir to the throne. I tucked the piece into my pouch next to the two rubies that had come from the queen's crown. The weight of such precious gems weighed on my heart as heavily as my responsibility to the royal children now depending on me for their lives.

"You must show this kind lady the quickest way out of the castle," Dot instructed her daughter as she retook the comfortable chair in front of the hearth fire where I suspected she spent most of her time.

The daughter hesitated and glanced warily at Dot.

"Go on with you now." Dot patted the knife on her lap. "I'll be just fine, that I will."

It wasn't until I was out of the castle and running toward the city gate with Constance in tow that it dawned on me what Dot had planned to do once we'd left her alone. She'd wanted to make sure King Ethelwulf wouldn't capture her and that her daughter would no longer have a reason to stay behind.

An ache swelled in my chest, and tears stung my eyes. I paused for only a second to look back at the tall tower where we'd left her, the sky darkening around it, the night beginning to fall. And I silently wept for the woman who'd sacrificed her life for me, for the princess, and for her daughter.

Chapter
6

LANCE

EVERY MUSCLE IN MY BODY TWITCHED WITH THE NEED TO RACE TO the royal residence and find Felicia. A thousand scenarios played through my mind—all the terrible things that could have happened to her, a young noblewoman, alone amid a city in chaos.

The sight of leather satchels wedged in the hay in the back of the wagon kept me from going after her as I wanted to do. But they didn't keep me from mentally flogging myself. If Felicia didn't make an appearance by the time the city gates closed, I'd have no choice but to continue without her. Saving the princesses was my number one duty.

Yet the thought of letting harm befall Felicia was tearing me apart. For as much as I'd silently complained about the inconvenience she was to my efforts to fulfill my vow to the king, I didn't understand why I was so concerned about her. Now would have been the perfect opportunity to leave her behind.

I told myself I only wanted to protect the young

woman from harm because she was attempting to rescue the crown princess. And I told myself I wanted to join her in that endeavor. But even as I tried to convince myself of noble motives, my thoughts tumbled together in a frenzied cyclone, and my mind filled with images of Felicia from the past twenty-four hours.

She'd been so brave and strong running behind me through the woods. She'd kept going even though I'd sensed she'd been ready to give up. And she'd set aside her own exhaustion on numerous occasions to care for the babes. Even now, she was putting herself at great risk to rescue the heir to the throne. My admiration had swelled with each passing hour of knowing her, and I was beginning to understand why the queen had entrusted this mission to Felicia.

I couldn't shake the picture of her sleeping in the hull. While rowing, I'd had too much time to study her features without her realizing I was doing so. Even though I'd tried to keep my attention from straying to her, it had, more oft than I cared to admit. Now the vision of her beautiful heart-shaped face with lovely lips and her long thick lashes fanned against her high cheeks was forever embedded into my memory.

I had the terrible premonition I was letting her penetrate my inner armor, and that I needed to fight harder to keep her out. Yet somehow, no matter how severely I chastised myself, I couldn't shut the door of my emotions now that it had cracked open.

Giving myself a mental shake, I narrowed my sights on a distant bend in the river, hardly visible from this eastern rise beyond Everly. But something in my warrior instincts warned me Ethelwulf's army was not far away now. If we had any hope of remaining out of his grip, we'd have to mask our scent and hopefully send his men in the wrong direction.

From Everly, the trip to the northeastern end of the Iron Hills was at least two days' hard ride on horseback. With a wagon, three infants, and a woman, I couldn't predict how long the journey would take. Accustomed to having everything under my control at every moment, I was frustrated at not being able to plan each detail.

I shot a look heavenward. Did I dare offer a prayer for direction? When I'd been but a boy, my father had taught me to rely upon God for guidance and sustenance. He'd modeled a life of dependence upon the Almighty, and I'd tried to imitate my father's devotion. But after I entered my training, and especially once I began to prove myself, I valued my own strength of mind and body so much that I no longer needed God.

Among the people coming out of the eastern gate, my gaze snagged upon a woman with a child braced on her hip. At first, I almost dismissed the pair. They appeared to be with a larger group of peasants who were likely returning home to the countryside with their unsold produce until the coming turmoil passed. As the woman walked, however, even with her head down and the burden on her hip, she held her shoulders too straight, and she moved with too much grace to be a peasant.

Relief swelled into my throat almost choking me. I slid out from the rock cropping where I'd hidden the wagon and started toward her. She glanced up occasionally, and I could tell she was attempting to search for me. But with the darkening evening, as well as the hustling of people leaving the city, she hadn't spotted me. I was almost to her before she finally saw me.

Her brilliant green eyes connected with mine before I

could drop them. The sadness there drove into my chest like the tip of an arrow. What had happened?

This was neither the time nor place to get the details of her escape with the princess. Not when the other peasants were eyeing us, likely wondering who we were. Even attired in my plain garments and with my head covered with a straw hat, my warrior status was difficult to disguise, every bit as much as Felicia's nobility was.

"Wife," I said loudly enough for onlookers to hear while allowing the accent from my peasant upbringing to lace my voice. Silently I encouraged her to go along with my pretense. "Where have you been? You've worried me."

I tried to glimpse the face of the crown princess, but the little girl burrowed against Felicia. Either the child was frightened or Felicia had instructed her not to let anyone see her face. Whatever the case, we needed to get away from the crowd before someone guessed this was no ordinary little girl.

"My dear husband." Felicia forced a smile.

Before I realized what she was doing, she lifted on her toes, braced a hand on my chest, and pressed her lips to my cheek. For a second, I was so startled I forgot to playact. I'd never been kissed, and I'd most certainly never entertained the thought of kissing a woman. A strange heat poured into my gut, stirring me so that I could only think about how soft and warm her lips were.

Before I could figure out how to respond, she broke the sweet, tender pressure and took a step back. Her lashes came down to hide her eyes, almost as if she wanted to cover up her embarrassment. And that's when I saw the dampness on her lashes. She'd been crying.

I felt as though I ought to draw her into a hug or pat

her arm or something. But of course, I was once again entirely inept at knowing how to interact. And I had no wish to frighten the princess with my closeness.

Instead, Felicia took the lead and slipped her hand into the crook of my arm. "I am ready, dear husband. Let us go home."

Home. The word struck me. Neither of us would ever be able to go home. At least not as long as Ethelwulf claimed the throne of Mercia. We'd be hunted fugitives, never again safe, never again able to live a normal life.

My chest constricted at the prospect of what would happen to my mother and siblings if Ethelwulf ever learned of my name and my involvement in the rescuing of the princesses. I could only pray that the many men present in the king's chamber wouldn't reveal my identity, but I feared Ethelwulf would employ every method possible to glean information from them. I needed to send a message to my mother and siblings, warn them to move, change their identities, and count me as dead.

As Felicia's fingers trembled against my arm, I realized with sudden clarity that her family would endure threats as well, if not worse. The women in the queen's chambers had known Felicia was running away with the princesses. Under pressure from Ethelwulf, they'd reveal her name. Her family, as nobility, wouldn't be able to disappear among the masses like my lowly family. They'd surely suffer and die.

My admiration of the strong young woman at my side swelled. And as I led her to the secluded place I'd left the wagon, I knew that I could no more abandon her than I could the princesses.

Once we were away from the crowds, I retrieved a

crock from the wagon. "We must cover ourselves and the children in grease," I said, removing the lid from the pig's lard I'd purchased when I'd gathered the supplies we'd need in our travel to the abbey.

In the process of peeking into the satchels and showing the babes to the crown princess, Felicia paused and raised her eyebrows at me.

"It will prevent tracker hounds from locating us." At least I hoped so. If nothing else, it would buy us a head start, which we so desperately needed.

Again, Felicia did as I asked. Even if she wrinkled her nose the entire time, she slathered Princess Constance along with the babes and didn't raise a word of objection. Surprisingly, neither did the little girl. Although her big eyes were filled with questions and sadness, she cooperated with Felicia and was quiet.

"For the rest of our journey, you must pretend you are a poor peasant child," Felicia spoke to the girl in hushed tones as she coated herself. "And you must pretend I am your mother and Lance is your father."

I'd shed my cloak and shirt and was in the process of rubbing the grease across my chest from a spot behind a thick bush, giving both of us privacy. Felicia's words brought to mind her brief kiss and made my stomach flip. Although I should simply consider the playacting as part of the plan, I couldn't stop a burst of anticipation from coursing into my blood at the prospect of Felicia continuing the pretense of being my wife—

A sudden shrill scream rent the air, followed by harsh shouting.

In one swift motion, I grabbed my garments from the ground where I'd dropped them. I rounded the bush, my mind and body slipping easily into warrior mode. "We must go now."

I didn't waste time putting my shirt back on. Instead, bare-chested, I tossed the discarded clothing into the cart, lifted Felicia and the princess next to the babes, and then jumped onto the bench while at the same time cracking the reins to send the horses into a trot.

I didn't look back at Everly as I drove the wagon hard and fast to the east. I didn't need to. I knew what the screams meant. Ethelwulf's men had arrived. They would search the city. When they didn't find the princesses there, they'd start the hunt elsewhere. I prayed we'd have a day's lead, but I suspected it would be much shorter.

"Let me drive for a while." Felicia's voice startled me from my dazed stupor. I blinked and tried to focus on the same blackness of night that had accompanied the past two hours of traveling. The faint haze of moonlight was erratic, coming out only when the cloud cover thinned.

Again, like last night, my inner direction guided us along the paths that crossed the wide-open Eastern Plains. The long canals cutting into the farmland for irrigation flowed from the Cress River but were too narrow and shallow for boats. The only way to traverse the plains was by foot or wagon, and I'd chosen a solitary route, one that would keep us away from the main traffic fleeing from Everly.

I shook my head, more to waken myself than to contradict Felicia. "Nay, I'm fine."

"Please, Lance." Her voice was like warm honey, too hard for me to resist. "How many days have you gone without slumber?"

I counted backward but couldn't remember when I'd last had a sufficient amount of sleep. During the past fortnight of battle, I'd slumbered and fought in four-hour shifts like the rest of my comrades. And of course, I hadn't slept at all last night or all day. It was no wonder my eyes were heavy.

"Are the princesses asleep?" I asked.

"Our *daughters* are asleep." Before I could protest, she was climbing over the wagon bed and onto the short bench. The stench of the hog grease permeated the air around us, but even so, my body reacted to her nearness as she settled herself next to me. I could sense her being careful not to let her arm or shoulder brush against mine. "If you will not allow me to drive, then I shall do my best to keep you awake."

"I'll keep myself awake."

"You do not always have to be so strong, Lance." Her soft voice made me want to lean against her. But I'd stood on my own for so long, I didn't know what it was like to rely upon anyone else anymore.

"Tell me about yourself," she said with the authority that belonged to someone of her station.

"Are you ordering me or asking?"

My question fell before I could analyze the resentment it contained. I'd always assumed I'd accepted my place in society, especially since I'd had the good fortune of moving out of my poor home.

Apparently I wasn't as content with my birthright or my improvement as I'd believed. Perhaps being in the king's residence over the past two years of service had only highlighted the great differences between the way the nobility lived compared to the austere conditions of my childhood, the same deprivation my mother and siblings even now had to endure.

"I am asking," Felicia replied after a moment. "Do you not think here and now we are nothing more than a man and a woman, that all of whom we ever were has been stripped from us, and that we shall nevermore be the same?"

"We'll never be equal, my lady. You'll always be a noblewoman and I a warrior. No matter how we may attempt to disguise the princesses, nothing will change their royalty."

Felicia was silent so that the crunch of the wheels against the long grass and the plod of the horses' hoofs rose to mingle with the ever-present night song of the crickets.

"Perhaps you are right," she said. "But I should like to put aside our differences enough so you can tolerate my presence."

"Tolerate?"

"You cannot deny I have irritated you from the moment I joined your rescue attempt. You would just as soon cast me over the side of the wagon than abide my presence."

"Nay, that's not true." My pulse sped at my need to assure her of my regard for her, but I didn't know how to go about such a task. I wasn't trained to woo or win women. I'd never learned to interact with a common woman much less one of the most beautiful noblewomen in all the land.

"It is true," her voice had turned low and raw. "You can hardly bear to look at me."

I suddenly loathed the thought that I'd hurt her in any way. "In the fray of battle, you're a distraction, my lady. That's all." My explanation sounded weak, even to my own ears. "What I mean is that I'm not accustomed to the presence of women. And I'm only attempting to stay focused on my mission rather than letting my attention shift where it should not."

"I see."

"You're a woman of great valor and inner strength. And you've earned my admiration, not my disdain." My confession embarrassed me, and I was glad for the cover of darkness that hid my face.

"You have earned my admiration as well."

Her words and their sincerity settled over me. Though I knew friendship was forbidden, I felt the beginning of it anyway with this unlikely candidate.

Chapter 7

Felicia

We stopped the next morning only long enough to relieve ourselves and the horses. Otherwise, Lance pushed us onward as fast as he could go without tiring the horses unnecessarily. By mid-afternoon, he allowed me to take the reins while he slept in the back for a couple of hours.

I didn't want to admit I'd never driven a wagon before since I'd always had servants to do the job. But I caught on soon enough and realized that on this particularly straight stretch of road, the horses probably could have guided themselves, likely why he'd allowed me the reins.

I was thankful for the wide-brimmed straw hat sheltering me from the sun. I'd formed a blanket tent over the girls in the wagon bed and was grateful for Constance's help soothing and feeding the babes.

Around us, the wheat, rye, and barley fields spread out endlessly. Occasionally I met another traveler or came upon a grouping of thatched peasant homes, but I passed quickly without stopping. At times as I drove, I felt as if we were the only ones in the whole world. I rather liked the idea and found I didn't miss court in the least.

In the quiet, I reviewed my conversations with Lance of the previous night.

You're a woman of great valor and inner strength. And you've earned my admiration, not my disdain.

Those particular words reverberated in my soul, unlike any compliment I'd ever received. And I'd had plenty of them. In fact, the men at court made a contest out of who could pay the most elaborate and winsome compliments to the women they pursued. As with most of the courtship process, so much focused on the outward appearance. I couldn't remember any person praising me for anything besides my beauty. Except now with Lance.

But Lance was unlike any man I'd ever met. Not only was he from a different class and from the king's elite guard, but he seemed to feel and think deeply, two qualities I appreciated and respected.

Over the course of the night, I'd learned about his upbringing in Stefford, another one of the Iron Cities. Although his father was no longer alive, he clearly loved his mother as well as his younger sisters and brothers, all of whom he supported with his income. He hadn't seen them since he'd turned ten and had been fostered out to begin his knight's training.

Nevertheless, he had fond memories of his childhood, of going to the smelter and working alongside his father, even if the work had been hard and dangerous. I'd been surprised to discover boys as young as eight worked full days in Mercia's many smelters and forges, melting down the iron ore in a hot and time-consuming process that extracted the iron from the rusty rocks and produced an iron bar. Lance had explained that the iron was then transferred to the forges where other tradesmen shaped it into the many items that made Mercia a wealthy country.

I hadn't expected Lance to show any interest in my background and my family. But once again, he'd surprised me by asking questions about my past so that we'd shared long into the night until I'd finally fallen asleep sitting next to him. When I'd awoken later, I'd been startled to realize I'd leaned my head on him and that he'd braced me with his arm.

"To keep you from falling off the wagon," he'd explained as he rapidly removed his hold and put as much distance between us as the small wooden bench would allow.

At a shifting in the wagon bed, I glanced over my shoulder to see that he'd lifted himself to his elbows and was peering down into Emmeline's bag. He reached a hand tentatively inside, and a look of such wonder and tenderness softened his countenance I couldn't contain my smile.

"Watch out," I said, "or she will hook you and will not let you go."

Lance looked up at me and smiled. My breath caught at the sight, at just how ruggedly handsome his grin made him, so much so that I couldn't keep from thinking about the brief kiss I'd given him last evening. When I'd seen him coming toward me, I'd been overcome with relief and had only planned to smooth over his awkward attempts to act like my husband, which I'm sure no one had believed, at least until I'd greeted him with a kiss.

Even so, the moment my lips had touched his cheek, I'd realized my mistake. Lance wasn't like the men at court who gave kisses the same way they did compliments. He wasn't one to play games or dole out his affection without merit. Instead, I suspected he'd reserve his affection for one woman who would have to be special to claim his heart.

I forced my attention to the path and the horses before he could see the nature of my thoughts, for he had an unnatural ability to read me. "You must have a pretty lady somewhere anxious to know how you are faring." I said the first thing I could think of, but once it was out realized how silly I sounded.

He didn't answer for a few seconds. "I've pledged my life in service to the king. I vowed to remain single until death or discharge."

"Oh." Somehow, I hadn't expected his declaration, even though somewhere in the back of my mind I'd been aware such regulations existed.

"And you," he said after several moments. "You've left a man behind, perhaps your intended?"

I shook my head and gave a short laugh. "No. I am not betrothed. Not yet."

"Then there is someone special." His low tone was much too serious and drew my gaze to his ruggedly strong face. He met my eyes only for an instant before focusing on my shoulder. I wanted him to look at me as an equal, to do away altogether with his respectful custom of dropping his gaze. But how could I convince him?

I sighed. "I did not cooperate well with the court-ship process. I could find no satisfaction in a match centered on outward qualities rather than inner."

"I commend you for that, my lady."

"Felicia," I said softly. "Just Felicia." Maybe we couldn't be equals, but that's all I wanted to be, especially for the rest of our trip. I didn't know what my future held now that I'd made myself an enemy of the new ruler. I'd certainly not be able to return to court if King Ethelwulf even had a court. I'd likely never be able to visit my home, at least not for a long while. I didn't know what I'd do or where I'd go once the princesses were safe.

"What will you do after we deliver the princesses to the abbey?" I asked. He'd surely be in a similar position, perhaps even worse. "You will not be able to return to the army, will you?

"No, my lady."

I wanted to correct him but sensed he'd conduct himself with as much honor as he could, no matter how much I implored him.

"Ethelwulf will slay much of King Francis's guard as a precaution," he said somberly. "Those he allows to live will surely be better off dead."

I swallowed my revulsion. "Do you think any of the men will be able to escape?"

"I pray so."

In the distance, clouds seemed to gather on the horizon, and I hoped we wouldn't have to face rain. Already I was weary from the past two days of travel. Rain would surely slow us down and make us more miserable than we were.

When we stopped a short while later, Lance fixed his attention toward Everly. He studied both the sky and the plains, seeming to take in every tiny detail.

Finally, he sniffed the air several times, and his expression turned grim.

"What is it?" I asked as I held Maribel and let her finish the last of her bottle. Unlike her younger twin, Maribel was fair, with lighter eyes and a slight layer of silky blond hair on her baby head. I had the feeling she'd favor her older sister more than Emmeline would.

"Someone is on our trail." Lance rounded the horses, his movements suddenly brisk and purposeful.

My pulse gave an unsteady thump. "Perhaps other travelers fleeing the city like us?"

Lance's fingers flew over the traces as he unhooked them. "They're moving too fast to be anything but our pursuers."

He didn't need to say more. I stood and rapidly situated Maribel in her satchel. Then I took Emmeline from Constance, even though she wasn't finished feeding the babe, and tucked her into her bag as well.

"You are such a good helper, Connie," I said as calmly as I could to the princess. I didn't want to frighten her, but the urgency coursing through me must have tinged my voice, for the girl's eyes widened and filled with anxiety.

I worked for several minutes, cushioning and securing the babes amidst their blankets. When I finished, I was surprised to see both horses unhitched from the wagon. Lance had condensed our remaining supplies into one sack and slung it over his shoulder.

"We'll need to leave the wagon behind if we're to pick up our pace," he said. *If we have any chance of outrunning our pursuers.* I could hear what he left unspoken, but I, too, refrained from voicing it. I didn't want to frighten Constance any further.

Lance hoisted me up onto the bare back of the first mare and made quick work of strapping one of the satchels in front of me.

Then he lifted Constance and the other satchel to his steed and mounted behind them. "I'll lead, my lady. You must push your horse hard to keep up."

Without waiting for my response, he kicked his heels into the horse's flank and spurred it into a gallop. I did likewise. Horsemanship was nothing new to me. Like most noblewomen, I'd learned to ride early in my life, and I could do so with dexterity. Nevertheless, I wasn't sure how long our mounts could keep such a fast pace without tiring.

As the sun began to wane in the west, I was relieved to realize the clouds in the northeast were not clouds at all, but hills. We were within sight of the eastern Iron Hills, which briefly filled me with renewed hope. However, after the fall of darkness, we had no choice but to slow our mounts, and my hope began to plummet. Under the clear skies, a half moon showed the range gradually rising higher with miles upon miles of open plains between the foothills and us.

The babes had awoken hungry, and we'd stopped to feed them and water the horses. But it hadn't been long enough to satisfy any of us, particularly the babes. We'd listened to their pitiful wails until they'd fallen into an exhausted slumber.

I wanted to do nothing more than bend my head and sleep too. But without a saddle, I risked falling off. So I forced myself to stay awake, rehearsing all the details I'd learned in my lessons about the history of Mercia from the days long ago when King Ethelwulf's grandmother, Queen Margery, had attempted to steal Mercia's throne just as King Ethelwulf was now doing.

Twins ran in the royal family, for Margery had a younger twin sister, Leandra. Rather than choose one of the twins to rule the land, their father, King Alfred the Peacemaker, had divided his kingdom of Bryttania into two smaller realms, Mercia and Warwick. He'd given Mercia to Leandra and Warwick to Margery.

For a while, the twin sisters had each ruled their kingdoms peacefully. Then Leandra had died in childbirth. Even though Leandra's infant daughter Princess Aurora had lived, Margery had decided that Mercia belonged more to her than to Leandra's husband and newborn babe.

So began years of Margery attempting to hunt down and kill the Princess Aurora. Eventually, Margery had failed. When Princess Aurora had come of age, she'd taken her place as the ruler of Mercia.

Since that time, Margery's heirs had never ceased believing Mercia and Warwick should be united again and that their family deserved to control both realms. Now Margery's grandson, King Ethelwulf, was fulfilling what he believed was his destiny, reuniting the land into the country it had been under the great King Alfred.

But at what cost? And who was to truly profit from such a move? From what I'd heard, King Ethelwulf was as brutal as his grandmother had been. Although Warwick was known for its beautiful gemstones and craftsmanship, the country had been suffering and dying for decades. Nothing good came from Warwick any longer.

Would the darkness spread to Mercia?

By the time dawn lightened the sky, the tall hills towered near us, their craggy peaks majestic above the thick evergreen tree line, especially with the glow of the rising sun behind them.

We'd begun a gradual climb in elevation. I suspected we still had quite a distance to travel before we arrived at St. Cuthbert's, and I prayed the horses would have the stamina to finish the ride.

"We have to stop soon," I called to Lance as Emmeline began to fuss again, this time with more vigor.

"We can't!" Lance shouted. "They're too close now."

I glanced over my shoulder, surprised to see that we'd climbed higher than I'd realized. The fertile Eastern Plains spread out in a beautiful coverlet of amber and chestnut and beige. In the distance, on the grassy road we'd just traversed, I could make out the figures of what appeared to be several black horses without riders. A second glance revealed longer legs, narrow muzzles, and sharply pointed ears.

Those weren't horses.

My heart scurried into my throat and lodged there painfully. They were black wolves, likely from among the wild beasts that roamed freely in the Highlands. Were these wolves chasing us? I'd only heard stories of beast controllers, the Fera Agmen, who had the ability to train wild animals to obey their every command. Rumors regarding the Fera Agmen told of their powers to read animal behavior and communicate with them so effectively they could be persuaded to kill.

Whatever the case, someone had sent the wolves to

track us down, and the deadly beasts wouldn't bring us back to King Ethelwulf alive.

I kicked my mare frantically, but she was lathered with sweat, foaming at the mouth, and couldn't go faster even if her life depended upon it—which it did.

Chapter
8

LANCE

I CHARGED UP THE NARROW RAVINE, SCANNING THE ROCKY BANKS on either side. "Go ahead of me!" I shouted to Felicia. "And ride into the abandoned mine."

The panic that had been building inside my chest over the past several hours of hard riding had swelled into a heavy stone weighing me down more than anything ever had in my life. I didn't have the time to analyze why I was so frightened. All I could do was react on instinct and training.

The crown princess had been brave all night and clung to the bag containing her baby sister. She rode low and hadn't made a sound except to soothe the crying babe from time to time. Already at three years of age, she was a girl I could admire. Someday she'd make a worthy queen, one I'd be proud to serve. If I could manage to keep her alive.

In the jagged cliffs above, I located the large stone I'd seen from afar. I slowed my horse and began to rise on its back. "Stay low, Your Highness, and hold on." I straightened to my full height and balanced on the horse's hind-quarters. Then, allowing the momentum of the steed to give me a boost, I leaped and found a foothold in the rock wall. Hand over hand, I climbed up the stones, using the crevices in the wall as leverage for my feet. When I finally pulled myself to the ledge where the large stone rested, I glanced down the ravine to see that the leader of the wolf pack had already bounded into the narrow passageway.

I didn't have much time, which meant I had to act right away. I shoved the stone, pushing at it with every ounce of strength in my body, the strength I'd honed and developed over years of grueling drills involving riding, running, swimming, crawling, and climbing We'd been trained to go days without sleep and food, all the while constantly fighting and exerting ourselves. In fact, the training was so intense at times, those who couldn't handle it died or dropped out of the king's army.

All the hard work had prepared me for any conceivable situation, including the possibility of taking the royal family to safety. While I was holding up physically, as I knew I could, I wasn't able to shake the strange new fear clutching my heart.

Don't let your emotions get in the way of what you need to do, I silently admonished myself as I heaved my full weight against the boulder. It slid, and smaller rocks crumbled away. I grunted and pushed the stone again, this time moving it far enough to dislodge it from the ledge. I didn't watch it fall. Instead, I shoved at the rest of the rocks of various sizes, sending a shower down with it.

The boulder picked up speed, barreling into other large rocks and knocking them loose until an avalanche of stones poured into the ravine and formed a wall between the wolves and us. The steep pile of debris wouldn't hold the fierce creatures for long, but it was enough of an impediment to give us more time.

I scrambled down and sprinted to catch up with my horse, racing until I grasped its tail. Swinging up behind the crown princess, I urged the steed to move faster.

If my memory of what I'd learned about the eastern Iron Hills held true, the old mine would give us shelter for a few hours, at least until I had the chance to explore the old tunnels and see if I could discover another way out. Otherwise, I'd fight the wolves to the death.

Ahead, in the flat side of a cliff, an opening beckoned me. Braced along the edges with beams, the door wasn't tall, and I flattened myself against the princess and satchel as I charged through. Felicia had already dismounted and stood ready by a thick slab of wood, which she began to shove over the door. The rusty bearings screeched in protest against the equally rusted iron track, and Felicia moved the door mere inches.

I jumped from my mount and pulled the door from one end as she pushed from the other. The metal scraped and screamed until with a final shove the door slid closed, shutting out the last few inches of light. I didn't know how intelligent the wolves were, whether they'd be able to figure out a way to slide the door open, but I wasn't taking any chances. I fumbled for a beam to wedge it in place.

Only after it was securely sealed did I stand back and attempt to catch my breath.

"Praise God the Father, Son, and Holy Ghost," Felicia whispered, exhaling shaky bursts of air that mingled with the heaving snorts of our mounts.

The sunlight coming in from the cracks around the door dimly illuminated the cavern. It wasn't large but was spacious enough for the horses. I'd figured it would be since the early miners in these parts had once used mules to help transport loads of ore in carts out of the tunnels and down the ravine.

I emptied the contents of our supply pack and located flint. In no time, I made a fire and lit a torch. "I need to explore and find a way out," I said as I started toward the main drift that descended gradually into the heart of the mountain.

Felicia nodded, already busy soothing the babes, who'd both begun to cry the moment we'd stopped moving. She'd taken bottles from the bags and given one to Princess Constance, and now the two fed the babes.

"The wolves will be outside soon," I warned. "But don't be frightened. They won't be able to tear through the door easily."

I'd hoped my declaration would offer some comfort to Felicia, but instead, the bottle in her hand shook even more. She looked up at me from where she knelt in the rocky debris. She'd lost her veil, and her hair had come loose from the simple plait she'd used for binding and coiling it. It now hung in long, tangled waves that begged to be combed back.

I couldn't take my gaze from her beautiful eyes, so wide, so filled with fear, and yet so trusting. I shouldn't look. I despised myself for my weakness. Yet for a precious few seconds, I allowed myself the pleasure.

"Tear through the door?" she finally managed, searching my face. I wondered what she saw there and whether she liked it. It was a strange thought. I shouldn't care about her impressions of me. Nevertheless, I wanted her to think as highly of me as I did her, for once again, I'd seen the depth of her character reveal itself during the hard ride last night and today. She'd endured my pace without complaint. Although she'd grown weary, she'd persevered as well as any of my comrades would have.

"You have nothing to fear, my lady," I said. "If the wolves break inside, I'll fight them away."

"Can you battle them all?"

"Aye." I wouldn't worry her with the fact that there would be at least three other wolves joining the pack within the next hour—the few that had lagged behind the punishing pace of the leader. I'd sensed their trail. In addition, I'd learned most black wolf packs from the Highlands traveled in groups of six. I would have to use every trick I knew and every ounce of training I'd ever had in order to defeat six. It wouldn't be easy, but it was possible. At least I prayed so.

The best solution was to find a way for us to escape, and I had to do so now before more danger came upon us. I lifted my torch and shone it down the abandoned mine.

"You are a godsend," she said softly.

Her words stopped me. Something shone in her eyes, something I couldn't name, but speared my chest with the desire to hold her.

A godsend? Had God sent me to Felicia and the princesses? Was He at work in bigger ways than I'd believed possible?

As I ducked low under the wooden beams bracing the cavern and started down the slope toward the maze of tunnels running the length of the Iron Hills, the urgency inside me swelled so that my chest hurt. I had to find a way to keep Felicia and the princesses safe.

The thought rippled through my body, pressing down on me with that same frightening weight I'd experienced before. And suddenly, I realized what had happened. I'd allowed myself to do what my commanders had cautioned against. I'd allowed myself to care about my charges rather than staying impersonal and objective.

Felicia and the princesses had become more than just my assignment, more than mere bodies that needed guarding. They'd become real people I admired, whom I'd gotten to know and was beginning to cherish almost as much as I did my own family.

In fact, I was chagrined to admit, even to myself, how often my thoughts had strayed to Felicia during the previous long night. Although I'd refrained from glancing at her over my shoulder like I'd wanted to, my mind's eye had vividly pictured her, especially the way she'd looked driving the cart yesterday with the sunlight spilling across her hat so that her face had glowed with a vibrancy and life that filled me with longings I couldn't explain.

"Stay objective. Don't feel. Keep alert." I chastised myself with the many warnings of my commanders. Of course, my first real interaction with a woman was sure to tempt me after the years of keeping my distance from the fairer sex. I was bound to struggle as many of my comrades had.

Perhaps I'd even been too harsh on the men who'd broken their vows of singleness. I'd rushed to judge them, thinking I was so much stronger and better than they were. The truth was that I'd just never experienced the powerful draw of a woman.

Until now. Until Felicia.

Ducking under cobwebs and loose tunnel beams, I shook my head and willed myself to stop thinking of her, to focus on the job of finding a way out of the shaft. My footsteps echoed hollowly as I descended. The torchlight flickered upright, without a breeze or breath of air to guide me to another entrance or opening.

Keeping my emotional distance from Felicia would perhaps be harder than fighting wolves, but if I had any hope of saving her, I had to stay aloof and simply do my job.

I ran through the tunnels as best I could amidst the crumbling rocks. Deeper and deeper into the mine I ventured, searching for an exit or for a safer place for the girls until finally, I reached a cavern that opened up into a fresh pool. I bent and took a long drink, filled my leather drinking gourd, and then splashed the ice-cold water on my face. Fatigue crowded in with every breath I took, and I prayed I'd have the stamina to find a way out of our predicament.

A search along the edge of the pool brought me to a man-made aqueduct. It had likely once carried water from this freshwater spring to a different part of the mine but was now abandoned and dry. It wasn't big enough for me to fit inside, but if I had to fight the wolves, Felicia and Princess Constance could crawl in with the babes and make their way to another level of the mine.

A distant, frightened scream sent a chill up my spine. It was too childlike to be Felicia's, and I guessed it had come from Princess Constance. I traced my path back, my heart thudding hard enough to bruise my rib cage, my thoughts an anxious tangle rather than the usual calm reserve. By the time I dashed up the tunnel and into the cavern where I'd left my charges, panic overwhelmed me at the prospect that the wolves had made it inside and were even now tearing the girls apart from limb to limb.

At the sight of them still alive and unharmed, I stopped short, my lungs flaming. Felicia stood at the door, knife in hand, and was attempting unsuccessfully to slash a wolf whenever it stuck its paw or muzzle into the fist-sized hole it had already dug through the wood. Princess Constance crouched next to the satchels, one on either side of her, squeezing them closely. Her expression was wide with terror, and she cringed every time the wolf made an appearance.

I handed Felicia the torch, then drawing my dagger, I bolted across the cavern. The instant the wolf poked its nose through and bared its teeth, I took aim and plunged my weapon upward into its mouth, killing it in one thrust. With a jerk, I loosened my knife while the creature crumpled away from the door, likely hitting the ground and providing a stepping place for the wolves that would take its place.

Felicia had moved back to allow me access and now rushed to comfort Princess Constance and the babes.

I studied the gap and realized the door wouldn't hold as long as I'd believed. I'd been gone for less than an hour, and already the beasts had chipped and broken away the rotting oak with their sharp claws and fangs. With all of them working together, they'd create a big enough opening in no time.

I crossed to my horse, retrieved my sword and flail, and led the horses to the far end of the cavern where they'd be away from the coming fight. I needed to take Felicia and the girls out of the way too, far out of the way.

"You must move deeper into the mines." Before I could give further directive, the door splintered, and a wolf leaped through.

Chapter
9

Felicia

Constance screamed again and buried her face against my coarse skirt. At the sight of the enormous wolf, slinking down and baring its teeth in a growl, I wanted to scream too.

The creature was the size of a grizzly bear, with its black fur standing on end, making it appear even larger. Its eyes glowed gold and blood-hungry. Somehow, the beast had managed to rip the hole wide enough to squeeze through. A second wolf was already pawing at the entrance.

We would soon be surrounded.

"Take the girls and run," Lance said without shifting his attention from the wolf. He crouched, his sword in one hand and a flail in the other. He'd already started swinging the spiked ball that was attached to a chain and short handle.

The horses were snorting and whinnying in fear, their eyes as wild as my heartbeat.

With the torch in one hand, I grabbed the satchels

in my other. "Come now," I said to Constance, trying to keep my voice calm. "We must be away."

The princess didn't budge. Instead, she clung to my skirt as if burying herself there would make the terrible wolf disappear.

"Follow the path always to the left and it will lead you to a pool." Lance crept nearer to the beast. "Find the aqueduct and crawl into it as far back as you can go."

As he finished his instructions, the wolf bounded forward. It snarled and nipped at the air, revealing canines that were at least two inches long and deadly sharp. Lance didn't react, but instead waited in a defensive position, twisting the flail methodically.

I crept back several steps, dragging Constance with me. She started to whimper, and I couldn't fault her. Being hunted and attacked by wolves was nothing a child should have to experience.

Nevertheless, I had to follow Lance's instructions and lead the girls away from the danger. The further I sidled toward the tunnel, the more my heart protested deserting Lance in such a dire situation. His comrade had already sacrificed his life defending us against the Saracens. The prospect that Lance was doing the same against wolves twisted like a knife into my side. I couldn't just leave him behind to die, not after all he'd done to help me.

On the other hand, my higher duty was to the princesses, to the vow I'd made to the queen, and ultimately to the future of my beloved country. If I didn't escape now, I'd likely fail on all accounts.

"Go, Felicia!" Lance called as though sensing my hesitancy.

I dragged Constance another pace, but at the cracking of more wood at the door, I spun in time to see an additional wolf, this one bigger than the last, climb through the hole. Without faltering, it lunged toward Lance with a feral howl. He swung his flail, and the spiked ball struck the wolf in the side, eliciting a squeal of pain or rage—I knew naught—before bounding up and skulking toward Lance again.

At the same time, the first wolf slinked along the wall and dashed into the doorway of the tunnel. There it halted with head low, pointing its growling muzzle at me and the princesses, clearly intending to keep us from escaping further into the mine.

I shoved Constance and the two satchels behind me and then unsheathed my knife. I had only strapped on the weapon when the head midwife had handed it to me in the queen's chamber as I'd been preparing to leave Delsworth. I had no training in weaponry and hadn't even been able to nick the wolf when I'd fought it through the hole in the doorway.

"I'll distract it!" Lance shouted. "Then you must run!"

Before Lance could put his plan into motion, the first, smaller wolf sprang at me, flying into the air, its golden eyes fixed upon my throat. Though panic flashed through me—especially at the realization that the creature was about to slice me open painfully, perhaps lethally—I straightened my shoulders and braced myself. Better me than the princesses.

In an instant, Lance took in the situation. His desperate eyes met mine.

"No!" He pitched his sword like a javelin. It ripped through the air. The blade pierced the wolf's chest through its heart and sliced out the other side. Even though life fled from the beast, the weight of it hit me. Its claws shredded my sleeve and tore my flesh. Fire rippled down my arm, and I fought not to scream from the pain.

The other wolf had launched against Lance the moment his attention had turned to me. Even as Lance swung his flail, the beast's fangs clamped into his calf. The pressure and the yank from the wolf would have swept an ordinary man off his feet. But Lance brought his flail around again, this time directly down onto the creature's skull. The resulting crack and howl were cut short with a slice across its throat with a short knife I hadn't known Lance had. Where it had come from, I didn't know. All I cared about was that the wolf released Lance's leg and dropped to the ground dead.

Lance stepped over the animal with a decided limp in his leg. He shuffled awkwardly toward the hole in the door, his knife and flail lifted in readiness.

I reached for his sword protruding from the chest of the wolf at my feet. The hilt was cold and heavy in my fingers. I winced as I attempted to wrest it free, feeling the strain against the wounds on my arm, but the weapon was embedded deep and didn't budge.

Lance peered cautiously out the jagged gap where the wolves had torn through the door.

"Are there more?" I asked.

Before he could answer, a snarling face poked through the hole and snapped at him. With quick reflexes, Lance dodged out of the way while swinging his flail against the wolf's head. It hit with deadly accuracy, and the wolf squealed in pain before dropping away.

Lance didn't take his gaze off the opening. "Work my sword free by wiggling it back and forth."

I bent, placed my foot against the wolf's chest. Gripping with both hands, I wrestled and tugged until finally the weapon slid upward, one bloody inch at a time.

While doing so, I felt an eerie silence descend. I stopped my struggle to watch Lance. He'd tensed and raised his knife, clearly expecting someone or something to come through the hole.

A happy coo rose from one of the bags and echoed in the cavern. Lance shot me a sharp look, a warning to keep the babe quiet.

I released the sword and hurried to the babes. Dropping to my knees, I peered into the satchel at Emmeline's face. Her eyes were open, and she'd kicked her legs free from her swaddling. She was squirming, and at the sight of me stopped to stare, her eyes so sweet and trusting.

"You may cease your fight," came a woman's voice from outside the door. "I come to you in peace."

I started to rise, but Lance held out a hand, motioning me to stay where I was.

"My name is Sister Katherine," the woman said. "I am a nun, and I come to you from St. Cuthbert's."

Lance chanced a look through the hole. At the surprise registering upon his face, I rose and crossed to the opening. I glanced through and saw the first dead wolf that Lance had killed, along with three others now lying on the ground. They didn't appear to be injured but instead were sprawled out as if they'd decided to lie down and take a nap.

A thin, middle-aged woman stood in the midst of

the sleeping wolves. Attired in a long gray habit covered with a scapular that blended in with the stones around us, the nun was almost invisible except for her pale face and gray-blue eyes the hue of a mourning dove. Even the coif and veil covering her head matched the rocky background. Only the rosary made of wooden beads and tied to the belt at her waist provided any color.

Lance lowered his weapons, unlocked the door, and then pulled it open, the joints again squealing with disuse. I followed, leaving Constance and the babes inside, not wanting to put them at further risk until I knew more about this woman.

When I stepped outside behind Lance, the bright sunshine blinded me for a moment.

"What brings you to our mountain?" Sister Katherine asked kindly but with an edge that demanded the truth.

"We seek refuge." Lance's knuckles were white around his knife, and his eyes took in every detail of our surroundings.

If anyone could help us figure out how to save the royal princesses, surely the nuns of St. Cuthbert's could.

"You have a little girl with you." Sister Katherine peered beyond me to the mine shaft. It wasn't a question but a statement.

"Our three-year-old daughter," I replied, unsure whether I could trust her yet to reveal the princesses' identities. "Along with our newborn babe."

It was her turn to study me, taking in my body and face, likely deducing I didn't have the figure of a woman who'd recently given birth, and concluding I was no peasant. Whatever her thoughts, she kept them to herself and instead nodded at my arm. "We should get you both to the abbey and tend your wounds."

Blood had seeped through my sleeve, turning the material a deep crimson. Although my arm still stung, the pain was bearable.

At the sight of my blood, Lance's brows furrowed above worried eyes. "We would be grateful. But first I'll kill the wolves so they can't chase us down again."

"There's no need. The sleeping herbs are quick-acting but will last several hours." Sister Katherine kicked at a piece of half-eaten raw meat she'd apparently laced with the concoction and tossed into their midst. "They won't be able to track us since I'll cover our trail with a dusting of mountain essence."

Mountain essence? My curiosity perked, but before I could ask her more, Lance was already spinning and limping back to the shaft door. Only then did I notice the way his calf-length boot had been ripped away and his hose stuck to his leg, outlining indentations where the wolf had gouged his flesh. The surrounding area was dark and damp, the blood continuing to seep out and run down his leg.

Seeing the direction of my gaze, Lance slashed the hem of his tunic with his knife. The linen gave way with a sharp rend. Then he wrapped the strip tightly around his calf, apparently to staunch the flow of blood. He did so with ease as if he made an everyday practice of binding wounds. When he straightened and continued, I knew that was his way of telling me he'd taken care of the problem and wanted me to proceed without giving his injury another thought.

Within minutes, we had the princesses and horses ready to go.

"You should ride," Sister Katherine said to Lance as he limped forward, leading his steed with Constance astride holding one satchel. I led my mount carrying the other bag.

"The horses are too worn," Lance said.

"Your injury is severe." Sister Katherine cocked her head toward his leg as though she could see through the mangled boot and hose to the flesh underneath. "And the climb is steep."

"We'll travel by foot as long as we're able." The lines in his face were taut, and a sheen of perspiration had formed on his brow. "I'll take the rear guard."

Sister Katherine pursed her lips as if holding herself back from admonishing him. After a moment, she handed him a pouch. "Very well. Then I shall need you to sprinkle a consistent dusting of this powder over our trail." Without another word, she started off, gesturing for me to follow.

The path wound through the ravine, and every plodding step up the gradual incline reminded me of my exhaustion. After some time, we came to a dead end at a smooth stone wall that rose steeply. I didn't know why Sister Katherine had led us to the secluded spot. Although a part of me knew it was far-fetched, my mind immediately began to consider dangerous possibilities. What if she'd trapped us and would now kill us?

I was surprised when she swept aside a large thorny gorse bush and stone to reveal a dark tunnel. With a gentle smile that seemed to show she'd known the turn of my thoughts, Sister Katherine disappeared into the opening.

We ducked inside, the horses having to hold their

necks low to fit. Lance carefully replaced the brush and stone before we started down the passageway. Even without a torch to light our way, a dim glow led us until it finally materialized into an opening that took us back outside. After again positioning gorse and stone to hide the tunnel, we continued upward on a rocky path that was hardly suitable for human feet, much less the horses. They stumbled and snorted, clearly weary and ready to collapse.

As my legs turned to hot mush from the exertion and my breath came in short bursts, I wanted nothing more than to climb onto my horse and ride the rest of the way. But every time I looked at Lance, I reminded myself to be strong, like him. His limp from his wound grew more pronounced with each bend we rounded. Yet he didn't complain, not even with the tiniest of groans.

I had reached the point where I wasn't sure how much longer I could hike when a bend in the path revealed the entirety of the Eastern Plains as far as the eye could see, maybe to Everly and the Upper Cress River and beyond. The view was not only breathtaking but disquieting. This nun could have been watching us for days. If so, did she realize we were more than a simple peasant family fleeing from Everly? And what would she do to us if she discovered who we really were?

Before I could voice my fears, Lance spoke behind me, his voice hoarse. "Felicia, you must sprinkle the herbs now."

I swiveled in time to see him sway. His eyes rolled back in his head. And then he crumpled to the rocky path.

A sharp cry of protest fell from my lips, and anxiety seized my heart for this brave man who could run for hours without tiring, go days without sleep, and fight multiple wolves single-handedly. He was made of a will and character stronger than the finest iron mined in Mercia. I knew he had to be near death to stop moving and protecting the princesses.

I knelt beside him, felt for the pulse in his neck, and prayed he was still alive.

Chapter 10

LANCE

I FOUGHT TO BREAK FREE OF DEATH'S GRIP. I WRESTLED FIERCELY with the black beast, slashing it and forcing it to stay at arm's length.

I didn't know how much longer I could fight it off. I was so tired and thirsty, ready to let my arm drop in weariness and my knees buckle in exhaustion. I wanted nothing more than to simply sleep, as I had when I'd been a lad still living at home. In the crowded one-room house made of wattle and daub with a thatched roof, I'd been safe on my mat in front of the center fireplace. I'd known my father was nearby, that he wouldn't let anything happen to me or the rest of my family.

Why couldn't I be that boy again? Walking in my father's shadow? If only I'd resisted his aspirations for me to become a knight and had stayed in the smelter working alongside him. Maybe then I would have been able to rescue him from the explosion. Perhaps I could have pulled him to safety in time.

Not only had I been unable to save him, but I was

losing a battle in saving myself. I couldn't remember anymore why it was so important to do so. Why not succumb to death's hold? What reason did I have to struggle so hard against it?

I tried to make my mind work. But all I knew was that I was fighting. Always fighting. And this time it was against death.

"He responds to your touch," said a wobbly older voice above me.

"If only that were enough." The reply was sad and weary. Felicia?

I was suddenly conscious of her fingers wrapped around my hand squeezing gently.

"Perhaps if you gave him a kiss," the older person said.

There was a pause. Then a whispered, "I really shouldn't—"

"It is quite clear you love him."

"It is?"

"Of course. You can hardly eat or sleep with your worry. And you have rarely left his side in the four days you have been here."

Four days? And where was *here*? Were we inside the holy house?

"Now go ahead. Give him true love's kiss, for it is oft the strongest weapon for fighting the battle with death."

Already I could feel my pulse gaining strength. Did Felicia love me? Surely, that wasn't correct. She was of the noble class. She couldn't stoop to loving someone like me. I was a nobody, only her protector, the simple soldier who'd been assigned to serve the king's dying wish.

Felicia's fingers tightened around mine.

Part of me cautioned my brain to do the honorable thing and wake up. But the other part of me was still too weary, too entangled with the grip of death to make the effort.

"I shall step outside for a moment to allow you the privacy," said the older one.

"Thank you," Felicia replied, her voice breathy with shyness.

Slow footsteps crossed the room with a plodding that confirmed this woman was old, probably on the heavy side, with arthritis in her joints. Once the door clicked closed, my senses awakened to other details of my surroundings: the scent of a dozen herbal remedies, the coolness of stone walls as well as the thickness of them that brought a solid silence to the room.

I could feel Felicia rise and realized she'd been sitting in a chair beside my bed which was a pallet of some sort, more comfortable than the floor but certainly not soft beneath my aching limbs.

The movement of the air as well as the slight sounds of her shuffling told me she leaned above me. If I opened my eyes, I'd likely see her hovering there, her green eyes filled with worry—worry about me and whether she was doing the right thing in following the nun's advice.

I needed to tell her she didn't have to do anything that would make her uncomfortable. That it wasn't her job to rescue me. That she didn't have to pretend to love me.

She dropped nearer until I felt her breath just above my face. Then it was above my mouth. And all thoughts ceased, save one.

I wanted her to kiss me.

For long moments, her breathing bathed me. It contained the fresh scent of mint. And warmth. Slowly the warmth spread from my chest to my arms and fingers. Then it moved from my heart to my legs and toes. Already, her nearness alone was giving me renewed strength. She wasn't obligated to kiss me.

My longing for her kiss grew nonetheless, my lungs searing with the need. I thought I might perish, until her lips brushed mine, sweetly and softly like a gentle summer sprinkle after a hot day of work.

I basked for several heartbeats in the refreshment and life that poured through me. When she lessened the pressure and began to rise, I chased after her, finally reacting, finally coming to life. I captured her lips in a kiss that came from all the emotion I'd felt over the past days. The admiration, appreciation, and aye, even attraction. I couldn't deny I cared deeply for this young woman.

We hadn't known each other long, but what we'd gone through together in saving the princesses had somehow formed a bond I couldn't deny. I'd broken all the rules of the king's guard and my vow of celibacy. And I'd broken the boundaries of our classes. But something swelled inside me so deeply I couldn't quell my need to respond and to communicate back my growing feelings.

I held her lips in a kiss that lasted only a few more seconds before she released the pressure and raised her head. Her beautiful eyes landed upon mine, making me realize I was fully conscious. Our gazes locked, and her eyes widened, giving me a glimpse into her soul, to the worry and concern she'd harbored there while I'd been delirious.

"You are awake," she said softly, letting her lashes drop to veil the embarrassment that had moved in. "How do you feel?"

I wanted to reach for her hand and reassure her I coveted her attention. But I couldn't make my hand move. "I've been unconscious for four days?" I managed, my voice hoarse.

"Your wound was severe." She glanced at the lower half of my body covered with a blanket. "And you lost a great deal of blood."

I flexed my calf, and fire shot through my leg in both directions. I couldn't hold back a grimace at the pain. "Are we at St. Cuthbert's?"

"Yes, and the nuns have been wonderful to us, giving us everything we need and taking good care of you."

"The princesses?"

"They are well."

"No one has tracked us here?"

"We could see more wolves searching the plains and ravines, but they turned back. No one has come since."

Relief hit me like a strong current. It pulled me down, and I sank into its embrace, closing my eyes and letting peace wash over me. I knew we couldn't stay at the holy house forever. I'd have to devise another plan for the princesses. But at least for now I'd kept them from Ethelwulf and harm.

I wanted to ask Felicia more questions, hold her hand, and stare at her. But I was too exhausted from my fight with death, so I let sleep claim me.

I slept on and off for another three days. Sometimes, when I awoke, Felicia was at my side. More often, the older woman was present—a nun by the name of Sister Agnes. I learned she was a skilled physician and had saved my leg and life.

The moment the wolf had sunk its fangs into my flesh,

I'd known the wound would be ugly. The teeth had ripped through muscle all the way to my bone. Sister Agnes had done her best to fend off putrefaction and repair the damage. But when I was finally strong enough to sit up and look at my calf, I realized I'd been very fortunate to remain standing and finish fighting the wolf, much less walk away.

"I have had a cane fashioned for you," Sister Agnes said as she entered the low-ceilinged chamber where I'd been bedridden for the past week. It was just one of the many small rooms of the abbey that had been carved into the mountainside.

Due to blending in to its surroundings, the hideaway was invisible to the outside world. Additionally, the route to the holy place was nearly impossible to locate without insider help. Although I prided myself on my sense of direction and ability to find anything I set my mind to, we'd been fortunate Sister Katherine had seen us and come to our aid when she had.

Sister Agnes handed me a well-crafted cane made of blackthorn. But I didn't take it. Instead, I stood and tried to put weight on my leg. Immediate throbbing enveloped my calf, so unbearable I had to sit back down, suddenly breathless.

"You need it, Lance," Sister Agnes said firmly but not unkindly. Her pale skin glistened with a persistent sheen of perspiration, even in the coolness of the stone room.

I shook my head. "I'll learn to get along without it."

She lowered her hefty frame into the chair next to the bed. Twirling the crutch in her soft, healing hands, she leveled a frank look at me. "You will never be able to walk again without a limp."

I flexed my leg and resisted the urge to cry out at the

pain that was still so sharp. "I'm young and strong. With time, I'll heal and be able to strengthen my muscles."

"That is true," she conceded. "But you will never regain the agility, speed, or strength you once had."

Her words pierced me more than the pain in my leg. Without my agility, speed, and strength, I'd no longer be fit for the army, much less the king's guard. Even though the king's elite guard would no longer exist as it once had, there were others like me who would never submit to Ethelwulf, warriors who would go into hiding—perhaps flee to the country of Norland to the north—until the occasion was right to fight for the true heir. When that time came, I would be ready to rise up with the rest of my comrades in arms.

"You must resign yourself to some other purpose in life besides the army," Sister Agnes said.

"I have no other purpose." I couldn't return to working in a smelter. I'd only put everyone around me at risk, particularly my family. As it was, I could only pray they'd receive my note encouraging them to hide, a note the nuns had assured me would reach my mother.

Sister Agnes twirled the cane again and then held it out to me. "Sometimes, when we think we've come to a dead end, we've arrived instead at God's stepping-stone on the way to bigger plans."

I wasn't sure I agreed with Sister Agnes. I'd worked hard for my position in the king's guard, put myself through years of intense training. I was a warrior, and that's what I wanted to remain.

Even so, I took the cane, placed it on the floor, and then rose, letting the sturdiness of it brace me. I didn't want to be dependent on anyone or anything. I'd stood on my own for too long, and it galled me I had to rely on the cane, on Sister Agnes, or even on Felicia. But for now, I didn't have a choice.

Before I could say more, the door opened and Felicia stepped inside. Her hair was windblown, her cheeks flushed, and her eyes bright. At the sight of her, my heartbeat began to ping like a hammer against hot metal. Of course, my thoughts returned to the kiss she'd initiated a few days ago. I'd relived it a dozen times, wishing it could happen again.

Ever since the kiss, she'd been slightly more reserved around me, as though she, too, was remembering the moment. But neither of us had said anything about it.

"How are the babes today?" I asked.

"They were awake for an hour this morning," she said. "The longest time yet."

Apparently, the first day we'd arrived, Felicia had admitted to the half dozen nuns who lived in the abbey that the girls were the royal princesses. She'd told me she'd had no choice, that the wise women had guessed as much the moment they'd spotted us from the lookout. A warrior and a beautiful noblewoman racing to safety together with two infants and a child? What other explanation was there?

I'd known we would need to divulge the information to the nuns at some point anyway. We wouldn't have been able to keep up the peasant charade around them for long. They were too intelligent and would see right past it.

Besides, we needed their help in protecting the princesses. During the few days of lying abed, I'd formulated a dozen plans for what to do next, and I always came back to the option of leaving the girls here at St. Cuthbert's. I hadn't been able to search the premises yet, but from everything Felicia had told me and that I'd gleaned from my observations, I guessed this place was safe than most.

Sister Agnes smiled at Felicia in welcome. "I see you have been out in the garden again. Princess Constance loves being in the sunshine, does she not?"

Felicia had told me about the large garden the women grew in a hidden valley within the confines of their mountain home. Sister Katherine oversaw the many plants they cultivated for food and medicine. Felicia had enjoyed relaying to me all the things she was learning from Sister Katherine about growing a garden.

"I did not come from the garden." Felicia spoke with a seriousness that sent a chill across my skin.

Sister Agnes's smile faded as though she, also, sensed a foreboding.

"I went to the lookout tower," Felicia continued. "A band of King Ethelwulf's army is riding toward the northeastern range. Sister Katherine says they will be here within two days."

Chapter 11

Felicia

I stood next to Lance in the tower and peered out over the wide plains. "There." I pointed to a distant spot on the horizon with a cloud of dust above it.

"Aye," Lance replied without taking his eyes from the view. "I never doubted you, Felicia. I just needed to gauge what kind of contingent and how fast they're moving."

"No wolves this time," Sister Katherine said from my other side. "But they will likely have someone they have coerced to lead them here."

"I thought no one knew how to find the abbey," I said.

Sister Katherine shook her head. "Other nuns know we exist. Perhaps one of them gave out the location not realizing the need for secrecy. Or perhaps one of King Francis's elite guards revealed our whereabouts and the hidden pathways that lead to us."

"Only a select few are privy to that information," Lance said.

"It only takes one," Sister Katherine replied sadly, touching the beads on the rosary at her belt. Her fingers were still covered from the soil of the garden where she spent much of her time, growing more herbs than I'd known existed.

I swallowed the fear crowding into my throat. "What will we do?"

Lance was leaning heavily on his cane, his face taut with pain and exhaustion from the climb up the spiral stairway that led to the tower. "We must move on and stay ahead of them."

I admired his bravery and dedication, but how could we outrun this army? Even before Lance's injury, the task of staying ahead of King Ethelwulf had been difficult enough. But now? When Lance could hardly walk?

The wolf's damage to my arm was healing well. Thanks to Sister Katherine's salves and poultices I doubted I'd even have scars. On the other hand, Sister Katherine and Sister Agnes had both agreed Lance would always feel the effects of his injury, an injury I blamed on myself. If I'd been more competent. If I'd taken the girls out of the cavern immediately. If I'd known how to defend myself better. It was my fault he'd had to save me at the expense of protecting himself.

Sister Katherine turned away from the window and crossed to a stone bench built into the opposite wall. She sat and waited for our attention. I gave her mine without delay, focusing on her slim face. Lance pivoted after a lengthy silence and then only reluctantly.

"It is time to do what we all know must be done," she said with her gentle gray eyes.

"What is that?" I asked, not caring I was showing my ignorance.

"We must split up the princesses and take them each to separate hiding places."

I started to protest, knowing the queen wouldn't want the girls to be apart, but Lance spoke first. "Are there three safe hiding places?"

"Yes," Sister Katherine said, glancing between the two of us in a way that reminded me again of the kiss I'd given Lance, of the way I couldn't stop thinking about him, of the way I couldn't help but admire him. His jaw was rigid and layered with stubble that shadowed the dimple in his chin. Even so, I knew it was there, had studied his face countless hours while he'd been unconscious.

He shifted, as though sensing my scrutiny, but he kept his attention on Sister Katherine. "I'll deliver each of the girls if you but tell me where."

"You and Felicia will take only one," Sister Katherine said with finality as if the matter had been settled long ago. "I shall take Constance to live with a noble family who is loyal to King Francis."

"Which family?" Lance's question was laden with steel as though he would strike down the plan without hesitation.

"She is a friend, a young woman who once thought to become a nun but then met her husband and changed her mind. I knew her when I was a novice at St. Peter's Abbey in Middleton and admired her. She has no connection to St. Cuthbert's, so King Ethelwulf will never suspect her."

"Will she be able to keep Constance's identity a secret?"

"She has three young sons and has always longed for a daughter," Sister Katherine said. "She will raise Constance as her own."

"But won't her friends question where Constance came from? Won't they want to know about her?"

"Unfortunately, once King Ethelwulf is done killing the nobility he suspects harbor too much love for King Francis, there will likely be many orphans. He would not be able to question them all. Besides, my friend and her husband live in a manor to the west of Delsworth. He will likely be spared from execution because of his isolated existence and lack of involvement at King Francis's court."

"And the twins?" Lance's knuckles turned white against the handle of his cane and perspiration dotted his brow, the sure signs he was putting too much pressure too soon on his leg.

"Sister Agnes will take one of the babes to another convent hidden in the Highlands. Even if King Ethelwulf decides to search every holy house in the land, she will be safely hidden until the danger has passed."

"Then why not take all three of the princesses there?" I asked.

Lance answered me before Sister Katherine could. "Sister Agnes will have an easier time hiding one babe versus three. Besides, if Ethelwulf locates and kills one, then the other two will still be safe."

I didn't want to think about King Ethelwulf finding and killing any of the precious girls. But it was certainly a risk, and Lance and Sister Katherine were right to split them up. At least for the time being.

"And the other twin?" Lance asked. "Where will we hide her?"

Sister Katherine again looked between Lance and me with that strange way of seeing deeper. "As I said, the two of you will take one." Lance started to shake his head, but Sister Katherine continued before he could speak. "She will be your daughter, and you will raise her."

One of the royal princesses? Our daughter?

"That's impossible." Lance spoke the words before I could. He lowered himself to the stone bench opposite Sister Katherine. His face was pale and his lips tight, either with pain or displeasure, I couldn't tell.

"There is an abandoned charcoal burner's house deep in Inglewood Forest," Sister Katherine said. "Many years ago, when Princess Aurora was a babe, she was hidden there for a short while to protect her from Queen Margery. The nuns who took care of the princess kept the location of the cottage a secret, and I am one of only a few who know about it. You will find refuge there."

Most charcoal burners chose a lonely existence. The job of burning logs into hardened black lumps of coal was hot and dirty and time-consuming. Although the many iron forges throughout Mercia depended upon the coal fuel, most people regarded the isolated charcoal burners with suspicion and left them alone. King Ethelwulf certainly wouldn't look for a royal princess in such a place. Sister Katherine's idea was brilliant.

But what about Lance and me? Surely, Sister Katherine could find more qualified individuals to raise a princess?

Lance was already shaking his head adamantly. "Nay. 'Twould be immoral living with a woman."

"Not if she is your wife."

Wife? Sister Katherine's suggestion halted my nod of agreement, and I froze as chagrin plummeted through me like an icy cold waterfall.

Lance's usually stoic face was an open theater stage, his emotion on display—first confusion, then mortification, and finally something akin to consternation. "Of course we can't marry. As one of the king's guard, I've taken a vow of celibacy."

"You are no longer in the king's guard," Sister Katherine responded. "You are a charcoal burner."

"And Felicia," Lance sputtered. "She's a noblewoman. We're forbidden from marrying by nature of our classes."

"The moment Felicia made her vow to the queen, she put a death warrant upon her head. She will never be a noblewoman again. As long as King Ethelwulf lives, she will be a hunted criminal."

I shuddered at Sister Katherine's blunt words. While I'd already considered the implications of my actions, to hear it spoken aloud and so concisely sent a pang into my heart.

"But a charcoal burner's wife?" Lance said in disbelief. "Nay, I will not subject a woman like Felicia to such a life. Never. We must think of another plan for the third princess."

Silence descended in the tower room. Outside the narrow windows came the echo of a distant hawk, and I wondered if it was a hunting bird sent out by King Ethelwulf's army. It reminded me we were running out of time. We couldn't argue but needed instead to act quickly.

Although Sister Katherine's suggestion for Lance

and me to get married and raise one of the twins was indeed shocking, it didn't fill me with revulsion. In fact, the thought sent a shiver of anticipation through me. I couldn't deny I liked Lance. Dear old Sister Agnes believed I loved him and that my "true love's kiss" had helped pull him out of death's sturdy grip by giving him an incentive to live.

Lance was an admirable man with many good qualities. In fact, he was braver, kinder, and more sacrificial than anyone at court. He was far and above the strongest and fiercest man I'd ever met. I trusted him with my life.

Yet, could I marry him? I studied his determined profile, wanting to look in his eyes to find answers there.

He focused upon Sister Katherine. "Felicia deserves a noble life with a husband who can give her all of the comforts she's used to."

The nun looked at me then, her wise eyes perceptive, her expression bidding me to speak my truest thoughts.

I hesitated. Over the past two weeks of deprivation, I'd realized how privileged and spoiled I'd been most of my life, how much I'd always taken for granted, how much I still had to learn about the world we lived in.

"What do you believe God's purpose is for your life, Felicia?" Sister Katherine asked. With her tight wimple surrounding her thin face, there was an angelic, almost ethereal, quality about her.

"I have been searching for it," I admitted. "I was not satisfied with court life. I did not fit in among the other noblewomen. And I longed for more than that shallow existence."

Lance's head snapped up at my revelation, and he finally met my gaze.

"I confess that leaving my comforts and family behind will be challenging," I continued. "But I shall not miss much else about my noble life."

"The charcoal burner is the poorest of the poor. The lowest class," Lance said. "You would go from every right and privilege to none. And for how long would you have to endure such a life? How long until Princess Constance is old enough to regain the throne?"

"She could do so at any time," Sister Katherine said, "since the throne is rightfully hers. But the old laws require a woman to reach the age of twenty before she can rule without a regent."

Lance hadn't taken his gaze from my face. "So we may need to hide for many years—until Princess Constance can legitimately become queen in her own right. Even then, she might not be willing or able to wrest it from Ethelwulf."

The queen had once told me we couldn't change every wrong in the world but that we could do our small part. Was this to be my part? To hide for many years? To mother an orphaned princess? To teach and train her to become an heir who was worthy of royalty, so that perhaps someday she could make a difference and help bring about another small change for the better?

"I can't ask Felicia to sacrifice so much," Lance said to Sister Katherine. "We must think of a different way. Perhaps Felicia can find safety with the noble family taking in the Princess Constance. And I will take the other babe into the woods by myself."

"You cannot care for a wee infant and support yourself," Sister Katherine stated.

"I'll find a pauper's daughter to marry."

"No!" I spoke more sharply than I intended, and Lance flinched. Taking advantage of his silence, I lowered myself to my knees before him and reached for his hands. I knew I was being bold. But this was a bold plan and one that would take courage for both of us.

"You should not be kneeling before me, my lady." He tried to tug me up.

"Lance," I said, resisting his pull. "Please try to understand. You shall marry me. I truly want to make this sacrifice for the princess."

His fingers closed around mine, the pressure solid and secure and everything I knew him to be. "Are you sure?"

I nodded and dropped my attention to his hand, already embarrassed by what I must say. I brushed my thumb across his knuckles. "I would make the sacrifice for us too." I couldn't make myself look up to see his reaction, but I hoped he understood what I meant.

He was quiet for a long moment. Then he caressed my knuckles with his thumb the same way I had his. The gentle touch made my stomach flip. "I wouldn't be worthy of such a sacrifice."

"You are worthier than any man I have ever known," I replied, admiring the strength in just his fingers alone. "And I would only pray that someday I might be worthy of you."

"But you already are—"

"If not for me, you would not be injured." The anguished words were out before I could stop them. "I

118

should have stayed in Delsworth and allowed you to leave without me. You would have escaped faster, and then you would still be whole, unharmed—"

He cut me off by raising a hand and pressing his thumb against my lips. The touch made me suck in a breath. His skin was rough and rugged, but I couldn't stop myself from relishing the contact.

"Nay, my lady." His brown eyes brimmed with something I couldn't name. "I was wrong to think you were ever a burden. You were a gift. Are a gift. Unexpected but necessary. I realize now I couldn't have saved the princesses without you."

"But your leg." I whispered against his thumb. "It's my—"

"Felicia." The gentleness in his whisper stopped my words. "Every time I think that I might have left you behind at Delsworth, I loathe the thought of what might have happened to you there."

At his declaration, warmth spilled through me. "Then you will forgive me for costing you your livelihood?"

"There is naught to forgive."

"Please, Lance."

"If you will forgive me for costing you your life of nobility?"

"I give up my old life freely."

"As do I."

I smiled then.

His lips curved up in response.

"Will you have no regrets about becoming a charcoal burner?" I asked.

"As long as you have none about becoming a charcoal burner's wife."

"None." And I meant it. Not just for the princess but because I cared about him too. I hoped he could read that in my eyes. I didn't know yet if what I felt was love, but it was surely something akin to it.

His fingers tightened against mine. "It will be a harsh life."

"It has already been harsh. But we have done this together, and we will continue to do so."

He released a breath, as though he'd been holding it in for a while. Then he reached for my chin, his fingers tender against my skin.

I glanced past him to where Sister Katherine sat only to realize she'd left.

He quietly studied my face. "And what if eventually you're not happy with a pauper's life?"

"I have no doubt we shall both have many adjustments to make in the days and weeks to come. We shall face hardships and danger. And we shall experience toil and sorrow. But happiness is a choice we can make no matter what life brings us, is it not?"

"It is." He rubbed his thumb along my jaw.

The caress was achingly sweet. When his eyes dropped to my lips, my stomach cinched with the desire for him to kiss me.

"If we would marry," he said hesitantly, almost hoarsely, "'twill be in name only. I will not dishonor you."

I searched his eyes, trying to make sense of his words. Did he think ours would simply be a marriage of convenience, solely for the sake of protecting the princess? Is that what he wanted? To remain friends and partners and nothing more?

I pulled away from him then and stood. We might

not love each other now, but we could give love the chance to grow, couldn't we? I hoped so, but I was not bold enough to say it. Instead, I walked to the narrow window and peered out, my mind's eye seeing nothing but his ruggedly handsome face.

After a moment, he rose and came behind me. I could feel his warmth close by, but he didn't touch me. "We have only a few hours until the cover of darkness and departure. We have much to do until then."

I nodded, forced a smile, and turned. "Yes. Much."

Chapter 12

LANCE

WITHOUT MY WARRIOR BRAIDS, MY HEAD FELT BARE. BUT AFTER I'd taken a bath and washed my hair, I'd refrained from plaiting the long strands, as had been my custom for so many years. Instead, I combed my hair until it was smooth and then gathered it at the back of my neck, tying it together with a leather strip.

I gave my tunic a final shake before leaving my chamber, hoping I was presentable for the wedding and wishing I had something to give Felicia as a token of my devotion. But I had nothing. And I was struck with the realization I'd never have anything, that instead of moving above my father's station, I was about to drop below him to the lowest strata a man could fall, as a charcoal burner. What would he think of me now if he'd lived? Would he be disappointed?

I could only hope he'd understand I was doing this for a higher purpose and greater good. After all, he was the one who'd told me that often sacrifices must be made without the satisfaction of praise from others. In the days to come, my satisfaction in laboring at a job I'd never asked for was that I'd save both the princess and Felicia. From now on, they would be my life mission.

As I exited into the dark, narrow passageway, needles shot through my leg with each step I took. My ineptness twisted my frustration tighter, and the *thunk* of the cane against the floor reminded me I was a cripple, that I would be for the rest of my life. Why would a beautiful, poised, and kind woman like Felicia want to marry a pauper and a cripple?

As I neared the chapel, my trepidation mounted. I stopped outside the door and wiped at the fresh perspiration on my brow. For an endless moment, I hesitated, knowing I should run away and give Felicia her freedom, that she should have a better man, a better life.

But at the soft tinkle of her laughter from within the small sanctuary, I straightened and rounded the corner. She was standing near the altar with the nuns surrounding her and fixing a wreath of flowers on her head.

I slicked back my hair, self-conscious.

At the sight of me, the nuns quieted and moved away, revealing Felicia.

All coherent thoughts fled and my breath hitched in my chest. She was beautiful. Her thick sable hair cascaded freely over her shoulders and down her back. Thin white ribbons from the flower wreath wound through the curls. Her cheeks flushed a rosy pink, and her eyes were bright. Even in her peasant tunic, she was stunning.

She offered me a tentative smile, and it beckoned me forward, drawing me, making my heart thud hard with all I felt for her. I didn't want to give her up. I couldn't. I'd never loved a woman before, but my affection for her already ran deep. I wanted to keep her close, protect her from those searching for her, and die for her if necessary. Somehow, in the short time I'd known her, she'd captured my heart. It belonged to her now and would always.

When I took my place next to her at the altar, the abbess placed our hands together. At the mere contact of her soft small hand inside my callused one, the seriousness of the occasion reverberated down to my soul.

"Wilt thou have this woman to be thy wedded wife," the abbess said. "To live together after God's ordinance in the holy estate of matrimony? Wilt thou love her, comfort her, honor, and keep her, in sickness and in health; and forsaking all other, keep thee only unto her so long as ye both shall live?"

"I will." My vow slipped out without hesitation. "Always."

Felicia's eyes rounded at my added declaration.

The abbess asked her the same question, and her answer came just as quickly as mine had. "I will." She met my gaze. "Always."

The solemnity in her eyes and her echo of my extra promise stoked a fire inside me, a burning need to pull her close and seal our vows with a kiss. But my willpower was stronger than forged iron, and I kept the proper boundary between us.

The abbess spoke a prayer of blessing over us, and then she pronounced us man and wife. The brief ceremony concluded within minutes, and once again, I wished I had something I could give Felicia to show her my affection.

But the nuns were dispersing, putting into motion our plans of escape. We had this night and perhaps part of tomorrow before Ethelwulf's knights arrived at St. Cuthbert's and realized we were no longer there. We had to take advantage of every second of the darkness to get as far as possible.

Thankfully, the abbey had a pair of mules. We agreed that Felicia and I would take one. Sister Katherine would ride out on the other with Princess Constance, and Sister Agnes would use the maze of underground tunnels. In the meantime, two of the other nuns would ride our horses and lead our pursuers on a futile chase, giving us more time to disappear and become lost to Ethelwulf.

Felicia had finally confided to me, Sister Katherine, and Sister Agnes that she'd named the twins Maribel and Emmeline. We'd agreed no one else at St. Cuthbert's would be privy to those names to ensure the safety of the princesses.

Sister Katherine determined Felicia and I would raise the younger twin, Princess Emmeline, because her dark hair resembled Felicia's. Anyone who saw the two together would hopefully assume they were mother and daughter.

While the nuns helped Felicia form a sling for the babe so she could carry her securely with hands free, I filled a knapsack with food supplies for us and goat's milk for the babe but little else. We couldn't weigh down the mule any further. Whatever provisions we needed, I'd have to fashion from the forest or hope to find in the deserted charcoal burner's cabin. The nuns gave us a few coins, but I would only use them sparingly in order to minimize our contact with anyone. The fewer people who saw us, the safer we'd remain, especially if Ethelwulf's trackers discovered our trail.

As we readied to leave, Felicia hugged each of the nuns who'd gathered in the courtyard. Then she kissed Princess Constance and Princess Maribel good-bye. When she turned for my assistance onto the mule, tears streaked her cheeks. She rapidly wiped them away, but more took their place. I gently squeezed her hand as I lifted her, wishing I could do more to comfort her but knowing nothing could truly ease this parting.

I groped for the small velvet pouch the king had entrusted to me. He'd told me to guard it with my life, that the contents would help the princesses one day reclaim the throne. Felicia had shown me the signet ring the nursemaid had given her in Everly and had passed it to Sister Katherine to take with Princess Constance. We'd also already given Sister Agnes one of the rubies from Queen Dierdal's crown for Princess Maribel.

But I still had this pouch from the king. I'd wondered if the contents likewise needed to be split among the princesses. As I'd packed, I'd felt dishonorable opening the bag and examining what was inside, but I'd done so anyway. I'd been slightly perplexed, even disappointed, to see three large golden keys and not something more valuable.

Granted, the keys were unlike any I'd seen before. The length of a man's hand, each appeared to be identical, with an oval bow and a long thick shank that ended in a fancy collar and pin. The only difference was that the bits on the ends of the pins contained unique engravings. I'd examined each one carefully, deciding that the little pictures must symbolize something, but I hadn't been able to figure out what.

No matter how regal looking the keys, I couldn't fathom how they'd help the princesses reclaim the throne. Nevertheless, I was determined to do as the king asked—to not only save the princesses but also keep the keys safe for them. I certainly couldn't retain all three. If anything happened to me, I didn't want to chance them all falling into Ethelwulf's hands. The best plan for their protection was dividing them among the princesses.

"Sister Katherine." I approached the nun already on the mule with Princess Constance in front of her. The beautiful little girl was burrowed beneath the nun's flowing cloak, her solemn eyes hardly visible in the falling shadows of the night. What must the crown princess think now that she had to race for her life again? Did she grasp the significance of her destiny?

I bowed my head to her in servitude and prayed the next time I saw her I'd be able to bend my knee before her as queen.

I handed Sister Katherine one of the keys. "King Francis gave me this key upon his death and charged me with guarding it. I'd like it to go with Princess Constance, to stay with her at her new home for safekeeping."

Sister Katherine took the key somewhat absently but then stopped short at a closer examination. "How many keys did the king give you?"

"Three," I said as I gave the third to Sister Agnes, who held Princess Maribel in a sling similar to Felicia's. With a bright moon overhead in the yet starless night illuminating the sleeping infant, I bowed my head in servitude toward the second princess and prayed God would protect her in the years to come.

"Then it is true." Sister Katherine turned the key over in her hand reverently.

"What's true?" I asked.

"The legend of the three keys."

With a large hood obscuring her face, I couldn't see Sister Katherine's expression, but her voice contained an awe that pricked at my conscience. Were the keys more valuable than I'd realized? Should they remain together after all?

"What is the legend?" Felicia asked from atop the mule where she patted Emmeline's back through the sling. Apparently, Felicia didn't know anything about the keys either.

"It has been said that the king or queen of this realm was given the sacred duty of being keeper of the keys," replied Sister Katherine. "But no one has ever seen the keys."

"Keeper of the keys?" Felicia asked. "For what purpose?"

"The legend says the keys unlock an ancient treasure that once belonged to the wealthiest and wisest king who ever lived, a man by the name of Solomon."

I'd never heard of such a king. Then again, my education had consisted only of what would help me become more skilled in warfare.

"God appeared to King Solomon in a dream and said, 'Ask for whatever you want, and I shall give it to you.' The king could have asked for anything he desired, especially wealth and a long life. But instead of these things, he replied, 'Give your servant wisdom and discernment as I govern my people so that I may be able to distinguish right from wrong.'"

Felicia nodded at Sister Katherine's retelling of the story as though she was familiar with it.

Sister Katherine continued. "God was so pleased with the king's answer that he replied, 'Not only will I give you the wisdom you have asked for, but I will also give you what you have not asked for: wealth and a long life.'"

"So the keys unlock a treasure left from the days of King Solomon?" Felicia asked.

"That is the legend, but no one knows for certain." Sister Katherine tucked the key into a pocket beneath her habit. "Rumor abounds that the treasure was brought to our Great Isle during ancient times to keep it safe from barbarians. Past kings have searched for it. Some have claimed that the quest for the Holy Grail is really the pursuit of an ancient treasure. Whatever the case, there are no definitive answers."

I shifted my weight, my leg hurting even though we hadn't yet begun our journey. "Then you believe the existence of these three keys lends evidence to the rumors of an ancient treasure?"

"It is possible," Sister Katherine remarked, drawing her cloak closer about her and shielding the princess from the night air, which was thinner and colder in the Highlands.

"King Francis said the keys would one day help the princesses regain the throne," I said, attempting to understand how an ancient treasure might aid the princesses. Would the treasure be vast enough to allow the princesses to buy the services of a large army, one that could rise up and destroy Ethelwulf?

"Maybe King Francis was referring to a prophecy in the Book of Dierum," Sister Katherine replied. "A prophecy foretelling a young ruler filled with wisdom who will use the ancient treasure to rid the land of evil and usher in a time of peace never before seen or ever seen again."

"We will pray King Francis is correct," said Sister Agnes, who rocked Princess Maribel back and forth. "In the meantime, each of the princesses shall keep one of the keys with her in hiding. And someday, when the time is right, perhaps the prophecy will come to pass."

"For now," Sister Katherine said, giving her mule a

nudge, "we must make sure the princesses survive. The ancient treasure will do them no good if they are not alive to find it."

I nodded and reached for our mule's lead rope. It was time to go. Time for each of us to do our best to make sure the princesses disappeared so Ethelwulf would believe they were dead or gone from Mercia. There would be opportunities later to sort out the role—if any—the keys might have in putting a new ruler onto Mercia's throne.

For now, though, we had enough worries, especially that of making it through the coming night alive.

Chapter 13

LANCE

I WANTED TO WALK AND ALLOW FELICIA TO RIDE THE MULE. YET soon enough it became apparent my slow, stilted steps would hinder our flight from the Iron Hills. I loathed myself for having to ride the mule while Felicia was forced to traverse the steep, rocky climb down the mountain on foot.

But I cared too much for her to let my pride stand in the way of our escape. She led the way while I sprinkled the nun's special powder of mountain essence and prayed it would keep Ethelwulf's men from tracking our scent.

By the deep hours of the night, we'd finally reached the foothills. Rather than heading south and entering Inglewood Forest from the east, I'd made the choice to cross the remote regions of the foothills and enter the forest from its western edge, as far from Delsworth as possible.

We kept to desolate paths, veering far away from any town or village. The more isolated we stayed and the fewer people we encountered, the better we'd fare.

Speed was no longer necessary so much as invisibility.

As dawn broke, I located a grove of hawthorn bushes near a clear brook, and we made camp for the day. Safely hidden among the brush, I still could not rest easy. So I took charge of Emmeline while Felicia fell into an exhausted sleep. As she slumbered, I caught several fish but didn't dare start a fire until nightfall so that darkness masked the plumes of smoke. Only then did we eat a quick meal of fried fish and hawthorn berries. After covering any evidence of our fire and presence, we packed up and moved on.

We journeyed for seven nights before reaching West Moorland, bypassing each of the Iron Cities. We didn't encounter any other travelers save a lone shepherd as well as a goat herder from whom we'd purchased a goat so we'd have milk for Emmeline. Even with so little contact with people, I insisted we travel only at night.

Purple heather, long grass, and sedge covered the rolling hills which were home to all manner of small game. I had no trouble hunting hare, grouse, or weasel. Bilberries, rosehips, and dandelions were also plentiful.

Each day, my wound healed and I gained strength. With the aid of my cane, I walked more often, even though at times the pain was unbearable. Felicia protested less to riding as the lack of enough proper food and the strain of our journey took its toll.

During the trek south, the openness of the moorland made me jittery, even under the cover of darkness. I drove us harder and faster, wanting to reach the edge of Inglewood Forest. The distant howls of coyotes churned fresh fear in my gut, and I prayed Ethelwulf wasn't hunting us with coyotes now instead of wolves.

My hope was that Ethelwulf's men had chased the

false trail the nuns had offered and in doing so lost all indication of where we'd really gone. So far, it seemed they had. Though I might never know if Sister Agnes and Sister Katherine had succeeded in out-maneuvering Ethelwulf's men, I never ceased praying for them.

Through all the hours of praying, I'd come to realize perhaps weaker men had an easier time praying than strong ones. In all the years I'd relied upon my own strength, I hadn't needed God's. Now I was coming to understand the truth of my father's claim that God's grace and presence shine the strongest in our humblest moments.

By the morning of our second full week of traveling, we finally reached the thick meadows bordering Inglewood Forest. We were too near a small peasant village by the name of Cannock for my comfort. Nevertheless, I couldn't resist stopping at a clear brook, especially when Felicia begged for the chance to wash in it. Since we'd gone days without the most basic of bathing, I felt the grime and knew she must too.

"Only for a few minutes," I said, guessing we would come to no harm if we took a small break. The area wasn't secluded enough for staying overlong, and I'd hoped to reach the cover of deeper forest before stopping to sleep for the day. But the sun had just risen, and we still had time to spare before we needed to hide ourselves away.

Her tired smile at my acquiescence made me realize how hard I'd pushed her, how once again she'd withstood the pressure like a valiant soldier. Although I admired her already, my respect for her had deepened. She was the strongest and bravest woman I'd ever met. Even now, as I cradled Emmeline in my arm, my heart swelled with a rush of emotion for Felicia I couldn't begin to name.

I'd turned my back to give her a few moments of privacy and so I could keep my focus on the surrounding meadow and anyone who might be approaching. But at her sharp intake of breath and a subsequent cry of pain, I pivoted, my knife already drawn. A sweeping glance around the grassy bank and the few trees told me we were still alone, and yet my heart doubled its pace.

"Something's wrong," I stated as I crossed toward where she sat on a rock next to the gently rippling water. Her stockings and boots lay discarded on the ground beside her along with the peasant scarf she normally tied over her head. She'd taken to wearing her hair simply, in a single plait down her back.

"I am fine," she said, although her voice was shaky.

Still holding Emmeline, I knelt next to her. She'd pulled her skirt and petticoat to her knees, revealing her delicate ankles and dainty white feet. Part of me said I was her husband and therefore had every right before God to look upon her. Even so, I cast my eyes away from her bare skin.

We'd maintained a friendly relationship during the fortnight of travel, working well together, and even enjoying each other's company and talking of many things. Of course, I'd experienced incidents when my attraction had swelled, and I'd wished for more than friendship. But I'd kept the boundaries firmly in place. After all, I'd told her at St. Cuthbert's I wouldn't dishonor her. And I always kept my pledges and would continue to do so. Even now.

I focused on her face, where she happened to be nibbling on her lower lip. Her beautiful, full lip. I could admit I'd been more than fascinated with her mouth since the day she'd woken me with her kiss. Her lips were so perfect above her delicate chin and framed by high cheekbones. Her lashes were impossibly thick and long. And her striking green eyes never ceased to slay me.

As she dipped her toes into the running water, she grimaced.

Her reaction forced my attention back to her discomfort. "Are you in pain?"

"Just a little."

Chancing a look at her feet again, I sat up in dismay at the sight of the red welts and blisters that had formed, some of which were bleeding. All the walking had chafed her feet, and she hadn't once let on how uncomfortable she was.

I passed Emmeline to Felicia and reached for her foot, this time heedless of the impropriety of her state of undress. I examined the raw, open blisters on one foot and then picked up the other to see the same. Anger swirled in my chest at the same time as frustration.

"Why didn't you tell me of your blisters?" My voice came out harder than I intended.

"I did not want to slow you down," she said wearily.

"You should have said something." I ripped a strip off my shirt and soaked it in the cold water before gently dabbing her wounds. A cry slipped from her lips, which only pierced me deeper.

She didn't respond as I tended first one foot, then the other. When I'd finally washed and dried them, I lifted her into my arms.

"No, Lance." She snaked one arm around my neck and clutched Emmeline with the other. "I can walk. Please."

Ignoring her objection, I carried her a short distance away to a ravine shaded by an oak, though my ruined leg protested at each step. There, I rapidly flattened a bed in the tall grass and lowered her onto it, helping to situate Emmeline next to her.

"Don't move," I ordered, knowing my voice still carried frustration but unable to soften it. I was too angry with myself for not seeing her pain sooner, for not being sensitive, for not taking care of her the way I should have.

I limped away, tended the mule and goat, tied them nearby, and then returned to Felicia bringing along her socks and shoes. She was lying where I'd left her, and her eyes were closed like Emmeline's. Had she already fallen asleep? I debated letting her rest, but at a glance at her mangled feet, I dropped to my knees and lifted one of them to my lap.

Her eyes flew open, startled and glassy from her exhaustion. "Just a little rest and I shall be fine."

"You need more than a little rest," I said as I began to apply the salve Sister Katherine had made for my wound. For long moments, I worked in silence until I'd covered her feet with the salve and then the bandages.

"I am sorry, Lance," she whispered. "I did not wish to be a burden to you, and now I have only made things worse."

The regret in her voice stopped my efforts to wipe my hands. I glanced up to see a tear slip down her cheek. Was I making her cry? I loathed myself for the hurt I'd caused her spirit as well as her body. Before I realized what I was doing, I reached for her, swiped the tear from her cheek, and then pulled her into my arms.

"You're not a burden," I murmured.

"Even though you are injured, you are stronger than I." Her statement ended on a sob, which she quickly cut off by pressing her face against my chest.

"Nay." My fingers seemed to have a mind of their own,

combing back the strands of her hair that had come loose from her thick plait. "I should be the one apologizing to you. And if I'm angry, it is only at myself for not being more sensitive to your needs."

She shook her head but didn't pull away. "You are more than kind to me."

I smoothed my fingers across her cheek and then the tendrils framing her face, the feel of her skin and hair starting to distract me from the matter at hand. "I don't know the ways of women," I admitted softly. "You must tell me when you have needs."

"But I do not want you to regret marrying me," she responded.

I leaned back then so I could see into her eyes, those mesmerizing eyes the color of the sweet meadow grass that surrounded us. I cupped her cheeks with both of my hands, surprised by my boldness. When she didn't resist and peered up at me trustingly, I was emboldened even more. "I will never regret marrying you. I would only regret if I had not kept you by my side where I'd know you are always safe."

Only at that moment did I realize how close we were, her arms around my waist, our faces mere inches apart.

Her eyes still filled with doubt. "But without me, you would have your freedom."

"Without you, I'd be desolate." I meant the words. If I'd left her behind, not only would I have gone crazy worrying about her, but I would have yearned for her companionship, her spark of life, her sweetness and thoughtfulness, and so much more. If I'd ever believed I was complete and my life fulfilled as a king's guard, I'd been wrong. After meeting a woman like Felicia, I knew now how much I'd been missing.

"Desolate?" She studied my face as though she still couldn't believe my words.

"Aye," I whispered. "Very desolate."

How could I convince her I meant what I said, that I didn't want to live without her? My gaze dropped to her lips, just inches from mine. Did I dare kiss her? My pulse sped at the prospect. Would a kiss reassure her of my undying affection?

Her lips parted slightly, as though in readiness. And when she released a soft, short breath that seemed to communicate her anticipation, I bent in and touched my mouth to hers. I hesitated, afraid I'd do the wrong thing, perhaps offend her. But her arms tightened around me, and she pressed her lips against mine in a kiss that let me know she welcomed me, that she wouldn't reject my affection, that perhaps she even shared it.

For an exquisitely sweet moment, our kiss lingered, making me breathless and lightheaded.

At a happy coo from Emmeline next to us, Felicia's lips curved into a smile against mine. I wasn't ready for the kiss to end, but she pulled back and released me, giving me little choice but to do the same.

She cuddled Emmeline closer, reclined in the bed of grass, and then smiled up at me. The invitation in her eyes and expression was like the warm summer sunshine pouring over me. A part of me warned that I needed to get up, move away, and keep the boundaries I'd established for our relationship.

But looking down at her and all her glorious beauty, the pull was too strong. I lowered myself into the grass, stretched out beside her, the babe between us. Propped on one elbow, I let myself feast upon her elegant features until finally I met her gaze.

I would not be so bold as to bend over and kiss her again. I'd have to content myself with simply looking.

As though sensing my resolve, she freed one of her hands, circled it behind my neck, and tugged me down.

I didn't resist. Didn't want to. Didn't know why I'd ever wanted to.

I kissed her again, this time for a long, precious moment. Until her lips stilled and I knew she'd fallen asleep.

Chapter 14

Felicia

My lashes fluttered with the first heartbeats of wakefulness. The air was warm and alive with the buzz of cicadas and the fragrant scent of Bridewort. I shifted only to realize that an arm was draped across me—Lance's arm.

I opened my eyes to the sight of his face near mine, his dark lashes resting on his cheeks, his breath coming in the slow even rhythm of slumber. Emmeline was cocooned between us, sleeping contentedly, her fingers wrapped around one of mine.

I wanted to drop a kiss on her fuzzy dark hair, but I didn't want to rouse either her or Lance. They were both resting so peacefully that I couldn't bear to disturb them. And selfishly, I didn't want Lance to pull his arm away, as I knew he would the moment he awakened.

Had he really kissed me? My attention shifted to his mouth, to his dimpled chin and his strong jaw. A swarm of honeybees set to flight in my stomach at the remembrance of not one kiss, but two. The tenderness of his gaze, the gentleness with which he'd bandaged my feet, the strength of his hold as he'd carried me to this resting spot.

As though sensing my wakefulness and scrutiny, his eyes flew open. I sank into their dark-brown depths, losing myself there. I couldn't contain the emotion any more than I could contain my thrumming pulse. "I love you," I whispered.

The moment the words were out, he stiffened and lifted his arm away from me, leaving me feeling suddenly bare and vulnerable. He glanced at a spot above my head, his eyes filling with regret and frustration.

Disappointment settled in, turning the air hot and stale and blocking out everything except the now heavy anxious thud of my heartbeat. The closeness and rapport between us evaporated as though it had never been, and a cool breeze blew in to replace it.

But why? Was it because I'd told him I loved him? It was the truth. I did love him, and I expected—had assumed from his kisses—he felt the same, was putting aside his reservations and finally wanted a true marriage. Though the past days of traveling had been difficult for a pampered woman like me who'd never had to walk more than the smooth passageways of castles, I'd experienced a new contentment with Lance that I'd never before had.

I'd relished the hours of talking and getting to know one another. I'd loved watching him learn to be a father to Emmeline. And I'd coveted every noble gesture he made for me. I'd begun to think God had purposefully placed us together, and that eventually

Lance would feel about me the same way I did about him. But he apparently still had no intention of allowing our relationship to develop into anything more than a partnership for Emmeline. We were only together to serve the princess and nothing more.

I lowered my lashes to hide my mortification. How could I have been so wrong?

"I'm sorry, Felicia," he said hoarsely.

But the distinct sound of voices nearby cut short his apology—an apology I neither wanted nor accepted. With his knife unsheathed and ready, he slowly lifted his head until he could see over the mound of earth. His face darkened, and he ducked back down.

"What is it?" I whispered.

He pressed his finger against his lips. I nodded and shivered despite the summer heat. We waited motionless in the grassy ravine for what seemed an eternity. When the voices were finally gone, Lance crawled to his knees, his keen eyes narrowing upon the surrounding area.

"Who was it?" I asked, sitting up.

"Just some children, likely from nearby Cannock."

"Do you think they saw us or the mule or goat?"

Lance stood then, sheathed his knife, and studied the meadow and woodland in the distance. "I don't know what they saw." Frustration laced his voice. "I shouldn't have dozed. I should have moved us to a safer, more private location before . . ."

He didn't finish his sentence, but I could hear what he'd left unsaid: *before we kissed.*

"This is my fault," I started. Normally during the day, we slept in shifts so that one of us could watch

Emmeline and remain alert for signs of danger.

He shook his head. "No, it's mine. I knew better." I wanted him to look at me and tell me I was worth it, that he loved me, too, regardless of the peril, that we'd weather it together. But his hardened warrior demeanor fell into place. "Don't worry. I won't let it happen again."

My heart squeezed with the pain of his rejection.

"We need to go now," he said. "Just in case the children saw us."

When he stooped to pick Emmeline and me up, I resisted with a push against his chest. "Do not touch me."

He quickly pulled back, hurt flitting through his eyes. But I was too hurt myself to acknowledge it. Instead, I situated Emmeline in the sling before fastening my shoes. My blistered feet ached at the confinement, but the salve and bandages had eased my discomfort.

I followed him to an area nearby where the mule and goat had fed to their heart's content and now rested in the shade. Again, Lance reached for me to lift me onto the mule, but I stepped away from him. "I shall do it myself."

Shadows darted across his face, but he allowed me to situate myself. Once I was astride, he regarded me with pursed lips, clearly waiting for me to look at him. But I refused to acknowledge him and instead stared straight ahead.

"Felicia," he finally said, his tone low and raw. "As a warrior, I cannot allow myself to feel for you—"

"Say no more," I cut him off. "You have made apparent enough the fact that you need no one but yourself."

He watched me a moment longer, opened his mouth as though to speak again, but closed it and grabbed the animals' lead ropes. He shouldered our pack of dwindling supplies before moving forward, his strides swift in spite of his cane and injury.

We followed the brook south for the rest of the morning, and Lance was more alert than usual, constantly scanning the area as though he'd expected the children to run back to town and report our presence. After traveling a considerable distance, we found a spot to hide for the remainder of the day before setting off once again at eventide.

The grassy meadows with a few trees gradually changed, growing ever denser until we were surrounded by a display of trees such as I had never before seen. Some were evergreens stretching to touch the sky with their pointed tips. Others were hardwoods of oak, maple, birch, and many I couldn't name.

Moss climbed up trunks, and pale lichen spread in abandon on branches. Clumps of colorful wildflowers blossomed in grassy spots. As we moved continually inward, the brush of nettles and elders thickened, making the way more difficult and overgrown.

When we halted at dusk to water the mule and goat, I walked a short distance away to a secluded spot beneath the low-hanging branches of a spruce. In this refuge, I sank into the soft scattering of pine needles with Emmeline to change and feed her.

Through the cover of branches, I watched Lance care for the animals, grateful for my position where I could stare at him unabashed without him realizing it. He tossed a glance over his shoulder as though sensing my gaze, but through the thickness of brush and leaves, I knew he couldn't tell I was staring—at least I prayed so.

No matter how hard I'd tried over the past hours to stay angry with him and to stop caring for him, I could do neither. The painful fact remained: I'd fallen in love with him and could no more stop that love than I could cease breathing.

The love had developed gradually and softly over so many days and through so many conversations, that it had finally come out whether I'd wanted it to or not. Now it would be a constant reminder of how I'd somehow failed to earn his love in return.

Lance stared downriver, cocking his ear and sniffing the air. "Men are coming," he called to me. "Stay hidden until they pass."

I scooted farther into the shadows, my chest tightening and a tired, dull ache pounding in my head. "Will you not hide with me?"

"I have nowhere to stow the animals, not with so little time."

After long minutes during which no one arrived, I started to breathe easier, hoping Lance's keen senses and intuition were wrong. But soon enough voices drifted our way.

"Good eve," came a friendly call from two men who rounded a bend in the brook, pulling behind them a cart loaded with wood. They were large, ruddy fellows with axes slung over their shoulders.

Lance stood slowly from where he'd been kneeling in the brook, his face a mask of impassivity. I could see that he was sizing up the newcomers and determining whether the two were friend or foe. "Good eve," he finally responded with a lowly accent and hunching his shoulders as he did whenever we came upon strangers to make himself less imposing.

After a few minutes of small talk and discovering the two were woodcutters, the taller of the men rubbed his long beard and narrowed his eyes upon Lance. "King Ethelwulf has put a price on the head of any soldier fleeing from King Francis's army."

"I am but a simple charcoal burner," Lance replied quietly. "Such news doesn't reach me where I live."

My heart pattered with a new kind of fear. Did these men suspect Lance was a runaway?

"Word has it that anyone who sees a soldier but doesn't bring him in will lose his working hand."

Lance didn't respond.

"I can't afford to have my hand chopped off." The tall woodcutter hefted his axe higher onto his shoulder.

"Neither can I," his companion added.

"I would rather not lose mine either," Lance said.

The woodcutters exchanged a glance. They didn't believe a man of Lance's physique to be anything other than who he was—a king's guard. Even without his warrior braids and chain mail, his broad shoulders, thick muscles, and air of confidence gave him away.

From the set of Lance's mouth, he was waging an inner war. In spite of his injured leg, he could easily strike down both woodcutters before they could blink. But he clearly didn't want to turn upon innocent men.

And yet, what else could he do? He couldn't allow them to run off and report him.

"Why are you passing through these parts?" one of the woodcutters demanded. "If you're a charcoal burner, you'd have your cart loaded for market."

What answer could Lance possibly give? From the way his fist tightened around the hilt of the knife in his belt, I suspected he could think of no ready reply and would fight even though he didn't want to.

I scrambled across the pine needles and shoved aside the branches of spruce.

Startled gazes swung toward me as I climbed out, stood, and situated Emmeline in my arms. "The babe's fed, and I'm ready to go." I attempted to speak with a poor woman's accent and hoped it was believable.

At my appearance, fear flashed in Lance's eyes. And anger. He'd warned me not to come out, and I'd disobeyed him. I was putting myself and the princess in danger. But I couldn't sit by and do nothing to help him.

"I told you to stay out of harm's way," he whispered.

"These good men won't harm us if we speak the truth." I hefted Emmeline to my shoulder and patted her back.

The men were watching our conversation with wide eyes, obviously not expecting a man they supposed to be a king's guard to have a wife and babe. I could only pray that after days of travel, the grime and dust masked my nobility.

I sidled next to Lance in a way I hoped suggested intimacy. "We're traveling home from Stefford, where I recently gave birth with the help of my family and a midwife. With all that has happened in the realm, my husband only wishes to keep me and our new babe safe."

As though sensing my ploy, Lance wrapped his arm around me protectively. "Aye, 'tis so," he said, the earnestness in his voice convincing even to me. "I have no wish to bring attention to my young family in these dangerous times."

The two woodcutters nodded, their expressions transforming from mistrust to understanding. "Aye, we know it all too well."

Lance leaned in and placed a kiss first upon Emmeline's brow and then upon mine. Even though he was only acting the part of a doting husband, the warmth of it went straight to my heart. "They're my life."

Although he spoke to the woodcutters, his eyes sought mine. The sincerity in the depths reached out to soothe the rejection from earlier in the day. He might not allow himself to love me, but he would cherish me. That I knew. But was that enough?

After a few more moments of dialogue, the woodcutters continued on their way wishing the babe and me good health. As soon as they were out of sight, all pretense dropped from Lance's expression.

"We must make haste. Now." The urgency in his tone told me we were not out of harm's way yet. That perhaps we never would be.

My body ached all over. While I'd endured much discomfort in the days of traveling, I sensed this was different, and I didn't complain when Lance insisted I ride the mule through the night.

Even though I tried to stay awake, exhaustion overtook me so that I slept in fits. During moments of wakefulness, my thoughts returned to the queen and the days I'd spent with her. She'd demonstrated such grace and kindness and peace in the way she lived. I prayed I would be able to model her attributes and train Emmeline in everything she would need to know as a princess.

Raising a princess was a monumental task. Maybe Lance was right. Maybe we needed to focus all our energy and attention on Emmeline. After all, she was our priority.

The queen's words of wisdom drifted through my consciousness: *Oft times we cannot change the entire direction of a route already set in motion. But we can do our small part to shift the path one degree at a time.*

With the darkness of the forest growing ever thicker and blacker, I bent and kissed Emmeline's head. Content in the sling, Emmeline nestled against me, which filled me with a new sense of peace.

I might not be able to oust King Ethelwulf and change the entire direction of the rule he'd set in motion, but I could do my small part to take care of Emmeline. By pouring my life into her, maybe one day my dedication and efforts would lead her to do something greater. I could only pray so.

Whatever the case, God had given me this role as Emmeline's caregiver. I would embrace the task and do my best to shape the princess into the kind of young woman the queen would have wanted.

In the meantime, I needed to relinquish my desire for Lance's love. I had to accept that he, too, was fulfilling his God-given role in taking care of Emmeline. Without her, we'd have no reason to be married. He certainly wouldn't have met me or spoken with me or spent time with me.

Emmeline was the only thing keeping us together. I couldn't let myself forget that.

Chapter 15

LANCE

WE TRAVELED ALL EVENING AND NIGHT, STOPPING ONLY WHEN necessary. My injured leg ached, but I refused to allow it to impede our flight into Inglewood Forest as far away from the woodcutters and the rest of civilization as we could go.

Sister Katherine had sketched a map of the deserted charcoal burner's cottage. I'd committed the route to memory but hadn't anticipated the path would be so overgrown and difficult to traverse. What should have taken only another day dragged much longer.

After the encounter with the woodcutters, I was more anxious than before to find our secluded home where we would have little chance of running into anyone. While Felicia's intervention might have worked this time, I didn't have faith that our charade would have the same results the next time we met someone. Too many others would also suspect I was a former king's guard. Upon closer examination, they'd also discover Felicia was no peasant woman.

We would have to remain anonymous and secluded for as long as we could. Perhaps for years. Thankfully, I'd been trained to survive under the most rudimentary of circumstances. But life would be harsher than I'd anticipated, and with each step deeper into the untamed forest, I regretted I'd agreed to bring Felicia into such an existence.

We said little to each other as we traveled. I told myself I needed to stay focused on the trail and prevent us from getting lost. Felicia, too, was quieter than usual, her attention fixed upon Emmeline. Although she regarded me with kindness and respect, I could sense a new reserve that hadn't been there before. It was for the best, I tried to tell myself, as was the hurt I'd caused her the day we'd kissed. Even if I hated that I'd brought her pain, it had served to rebuild the boundaries between us.

I love you. Felicia's words came back unbidden all too often, as did the memory of our kisses. But each time I reminded myself of the danger in feeling things for her. My commanders had been right when they'd said such emotions made soldiers weak. That's what had happened when I'd allowed myself to kiss Felicia and luxuriate in her nearness. I'd dozed and put her and Emmeline at great risk. The children playing nearby could have discovered us. Moreover, we most certainly would have been hidden before meeting the woodcutters. Even now, I feared the men had figured out my true identity and alerted Ethelwulf.

Aye, we'd all be better off if I put all thoughts of loving Felicia from my mind and if she did likewise.

By mid-morning of our second day of pushing deeper into the forestland, I finally found the steep ravine Sister Katherine had mentioned. The rocks lengthened in both directions and seemed impassable. I had to examine every crevice before I found the cavern hidden behind hanging ivy. Following the nun's careful instructions, we made our way through the cave and its narrow passageway, which eventually led uphill and opened onto the opposite side of the gorge.

I realized then that the rocky area would serve as a natural barrier for anyone who might search for us. At the very least, it would shield us from most wanderers and keep us secluded.

After several more hours, we stumbled upon an overgrown clearing. At the sight of an abandoned—though severely dilapidated—cottage I nearly fell to my knees in relief. It was concealed by blackthorn and covered by ivy so that it blended in with the woodland, making it the perfect hiding place.

"We're here." I led the mule and goat past a well that appeared to contain water.

Felicia's shoulders were slumped and her head bent, and she'd tied herself to the pommel to keep from slipping off. With one arm cradling Emmeline in the sling and the other tangled in the mule's mane, she slowly lifted her head. She blinked but couldn't seem to focus. Her head drooped again, and this time she started to slide sideways off the mule. The rope around her arm caught her and dug into her sleeve, keeping her astride.

Something wasn't right, and my pulse began to knock a dreadful beat. I rushed to her side, and the moment I touched her, I realized she was burning up with fever.

I worked frantically day and night in my attempts to save Felicia, but she remained feverish. My only guess was that she'd eaten or drunk something her delicate body hadn't been able to handle. I'd seen roughened soldiers waste away under the same conditions, nothing to be done for them except pray.

I rebuked myself for not having noticed Felicia's malady sooner, but I'd been so focused on trying to get us out of harm's way that I'd once again neglected her well-being, not that I could have done much to prevent the illness from spreading into her body. At least I could have made her more comfortable.

Thankfully, the cottage provided basic accommo-dations. Although the structure needed many repairs, Sister Katherine had been correct in saying it was well built and sturdy. The upper level was a dormer loft filled with nothing more than cobwebs and raccoon nests, as well as an abandoned loom.

The main floor consisted of two rooms—a bed chamber and a larger living area with a spacious hearth, trestle table with benches, several rickety stools, and a cabinet that was falling apart but that I would easily be able to fix.

With the chinking between the stones crumbling away, the interior wall gave up its secret too easily, and I discovered a hidden cupboard. After cutting open the lock, I'd been surprised to find a wealth of books and scrolls. Except for yellowing and brittle pages, they'd withstood the passing of time and would hopefully keep us company in the days and years to come.

Unfortunately, the linens and other woven items hadn't fared as well. Mice and moth had chewed through many of the rugs, towels, and blankets that appeared to have once been of solid construction. Tableware and crocks were chipped. Pots and pans were rusted.

With some scrubbing, I was able to clean one pot enough to heat water to boiling. More than anything, I was thankful for the wild, overgrown remains of an herb garden with medicinal plants at full growth, some of which I recognized and could use in teas and decoctions.

Between caring for Emmeline and Felicia, I slept and ate little. As Felicia thrashed in her delirium and began to fade, desperation took residence in my heart. I sat long hours by her side, holding her in one arm and Emmeline in the other. Though I had done everything I could to save Felicia and everything I'd ever learned about caring for the sick, I could do no more.

My helplessness galled me. I was accustomed to success—to being the strong one, always protecting, always saving, always knowing what to do. Yet I now found myself in a strange new situation where all my efforts were for naught. Neither my soldier's training nor my strength could save Felicia.

She shuddered in my arms, her body convulsing with chills.

I gently placed Emmeline into a nearby crate I'd lined with fresh leaves and grass. Then I pulled Felicia against me on my pallet in front of the hearth, cradling her, wanting to soothe her. I brushed a kiss against her hot forehead, wishing I could take her fever into my own body, wanting to suffer for her.

"God," I whispered as I stared unseeingly at the glowing coals. "I haven't wanted to rely upon anyone, have only leaned upon my own strength and determination. But I have nothing left. I can do no more."

The admission brought the sting of heat to the back of

my eyes. I'd tried to be strong enough for all of us, but in my own strength I'd failed.

My thoughts returned to my father, to something he'd said after one particularly hard day at the smelter. We'd had to stand helplessly by while another worker was blasted by an exploding furnace, covered in hot slag, and roasted alive beneath the bright-orange coating.

I'd been young and angry and questioned how my father could endure his own suffering in addition to watching others suffer day after day. "How can you stand it?" I'd asked.

"I can't stand in my own strength," he'd replied. "We were never meant to live in our own strength alone."

I knew now as I'd known then that my father depended upon God for strength and guidance in a way I never had. Was this what it took? Coming to the end of my own strength before I'd finally learn I needed more than what I had?

I buried my face in Felicia's long hair.

Not only did I need God's power to help me stand strong in the face of adversity, but I needed others too. I needed Felicia.

You have made apparent enough the fact that you need no one but yourself. Her words came back to taunt me.

"I was wrong," I said against her ear. "I do need you."

If she would but awaken and live, I vowed I'd show her my need for her.

"Please." I wrapped her in my arms, praying my strength would flow through her. "Return to me."

The ache in my chest had been swelling with each passing day, and now it pressed hard against my lungs and rib cage. I couldn't bear the thought of losing Felicia, of not having her in my life, of living here alone with only Emmeline.

I could no longer deny the truth. I loved Felicia. And I should have told her so the day she'd made her declaration to me. In fact, I should have told her the day I'd married her. Even more, I should have said the words when she'd awakened me with her kiss when I'd been fighting off death's hold.

Sister Agnes had called it "true love's kiss." I didn't know if such a kiss was somehow enchanted. More likely the kiss was a summoning, a beckoning, a pleading that resonated deep within the soul of the dying, urging that person to fight back and return to the arms of the one giving the kiss.

I leaned away from Felicia so I could see her face. Her dark lashes rested against pale cheeks. I'd do anything to see her beautiful green eyes one more time. If for no other reason, I needed to awaken her for a last moment to tell her I loved her. She deserved at least that.

With the swell of emotion rising into my throat, I bent and pressed my lips against hers. She didn't move, and I didn't expect her to. Nevertheless, I kissed her with the love I'd harbored but had been too afraid to acknowledge because I'd been too cowardly to admit my need for her.

At some point, the kiss deepened. I wasn't sure when I realized she was responding, that her lips had melded to mine and that she was kissing me back with a fervor almost as desperate as mine.

As the awareness of her consciousness penetrated my haze, I broke the kiss. My breathing labored as I examined her.

"Do not stop," she whispered before her lashes slowly rose. Though tired, her eyes were clear and tender. And utterly beautiful.

I ran my fingers over her face. Although she was

flushed, I could sense a change in her body. Even if she was still listless, her shivering had ceased. I dropped my fingers to the pulse in her neck. Though it was weak, it was thudding steadier.

My throat constricted. She'd listened to me and had come back. I forced out the words I could no longer contain. "I love you."

Her eyes widened. "You do not have to say it—"

"I have loved you since the first time you kissed me," I admitted. "I was wrong not to tell you. And I was wrong not to act upon it. But if you stay with me, I'll never again make that mistake."

"But Emmeline, she's our priority—"

"And she still will be," I assured her.

"I understand that you don't want to be distracted from your task."

"God's shown me I was never meant to do this by myself, in my own strength."

Felicia examined my face as though she needed to test the sincerity of what I was saying. I could only pray she'd find what she was looking for there. I'd pushed her away, and I didn't deserve to have her again, but I was determined to win her and this time keep her.

"What if our love for each other makes us stronger together?" I asked, voicing a question even though I already knew the answer. "And what if our love for each other will only make Emmeline all the stronger and happier?"

She hesitated. "If Emmeline left us today, would you still want to be with me?"

"Aye. Always."

"Truly?"

I nodded. "God brought us together for her sake. If the

day comes when she no longer needs us, then He'll have something different for us to do. Together."

She smiled. Though it was weak, it was the most beautiful sight in the world. She studied me a moment before glancing around the darkened room, illuminated only by the soft glow of the dying fire. The cottage was still dusty and full of cobwebs and falling apart in many places.

Anxiety pinched my lungs. With this first glimpse of our new home, would she regret coming with me to be a charcoal burner's wife? Now faced with the reality of our poverty, deprivation, and isolation, would she resent me and this new life?

"Our new home," she said softly.

"It's in disarray. But it's bigger and has more than I thought it would. I'll be able to repair and make most things workable in time."

She pushed up to one elbow and scanned the room until her gaze came to rest upon Emmeline in her crate next to us. She watched the little girl's sleeping face before dropping back to the pallet and closing her eyes.

My airways constricted even further. What else could I say to reassure Felicia? "I promise I'll do everything I can to make you and Emmeline happy."

Her eyes opened and met mine. "I am already happy."

"But this place . . ."

"As long as we are together, I shall not need anything else. You are all I need."

Relief and joy welled up deep inside, and I whispered a silent prayer of gratitude that God had granted me another chance to do things right. "Aye. And I need you. I don't want to live without you." The words didn't come easily, but I knew them to be true. I not only *wanted* her, but I *needed* her.

At my confession, her lips curved into a smile. "I must be dreaming."

"Nay." I caressed her cheek. "This is no dream."

"You are right. This is no dream," she teased softly. "Rather, I believe I have died and gone to heaven."

I grinned, my chest expanding with love. "Are you saying that lying in my arms is heavenly?"

"Perhaps," she bantered.

"You don't sound confident."

"If you would like my confidence to grow, there is one thing to help it along."

"And what is that?" I caressed her other cheek.

"You must kiss me again. And again."

I bent in and brushed my nose against hers. "I can do that, my lady," I whispered. And then I met her lips and showed her that I could. And that I would. Always.

Chapter 16

King Ethelwulf

I sat on the throne. *My* throne. Right where I belonged. I fingered the cool gold overlay and imagined my great-grandfather, King Alfred the Peacemaker, smiling down on me from heaven. He would be satisfied a rightful heir had taken the throne after decades of usurpers.

The great hall of Delsworth, the old capital city of the once united kingdom of Bryttania, was not anything special. The tall walls were washed in dull white lime, and the tapestries that hung throughout the hall were too plain. The rushes on the floor were old. The hounds too skinny. And the food bland.

Soon a ship bringing my wife and infant sons would arrive. And the new and rightful queen would decorate the royal residence befitting my status as ruler of Mercia and Warwick.

I'd call myself King Ethelwulf the Great since I had been the one to reunite the country and would return it to the world leader and power it had once been, especially after I located the ancient Solomon's treasure. Not only would I be the strongest leader, but with the treasure, I would become the wisest, wealthiest, and healthiest in the world.

The problem was I couldn't find the keys to the treasure anywhere. I'd had every royal residence meticulously searched, and I still couldn't locate the keys. I'd begun to fear the usurper king had destroyed them when he'd realized he was conquered.

The line of Mercia's nobility waiting to pay me homage stretched down the length of the hall and out the doors. They were a quiet lot and feared me, as they rightly should. As with any new ruler, I had to command order and loyalty from the highest in the land down to the lowliest. If my measures were strict and at times deadly, it was only to ensure my great-grandfather's kingdom would thrive and grow even more powerful.

I nodded, the indication my guard should usher the next nobleman up the dais into my presence. My scribe would read me the information he'd collected about the noble family and I'd listen to the nobleman defend himself as well as share how he planned to contribute to the newly united kingdom. Then I'd make my decision on whether to allow the nobleman and his family to live.

My executioners had been busy over the past weeks. Though I'd heard whispers the streets of Delsworth ran red with the blood of the people I'd condemned, such pruning was necessary for the stability of the kingdom. Besides, most of the convicted had been captured soldiers and the king's elite guard. There was no question such warriors had to be eliminated. I couldn't chance keeping a single one alive. Nor could I allow anyone who defended or sheltered a soldier to go unpunished.

The only way to ensure I would be able to pass on the

united kingdom to my heirs was to eradicate any loyalty to the old ruler whose name I would no longer allow to be uttered in any corner of the realm.

And of course, I needed to eradicate the princesses. All three of them. Which was proving more difficult than I'd anticipated.

The nobleman at the front of the line stepped forward and bowed to the ground at the base of the dais. Before he could rise, the captain of my guard, Theobald, entered from a side door and approached the throne. Several guards followed behind him dragging a prisoner between them.

"Your Majesty." The captain bowed, his black chain mail clinking. His shoulder-length hair was braided into three strands beneath his hood. When he lifted his head, he didn't meet my gaze but instead stared straight ahead, his face impassive. With the scar running the length of his cheek and disappearing into his sharply pointed black beard, the captain had the bearings of a fierce, brutal man. Just the kind of leader I needed in charge of my army.

"What news, captain?" I peered beyond him to the soldiers. "I hope you finally have word of the whereabouts of the usurper's heirs." My best guards had tracked the princesses to a hidden mountain abbey, but by the time they'd arrived, the princesses were gone. Apparently, without a trace. The special tracking hounds and even the Highland wolves hadn't been able to pick up a new trail.

I'd punished the guards for failing to find the princesses. I'd needed to make an example of what would happen to those who disappointed me. Now without a trail to pursue, we'd been left to speculate, which had proved futile as well.

"Your Majesty," the captain responded. "We believe we've found someone who can provide information as to the location of the princesses."

"Hopefully not another fool attempting to ingratiate themselves to me." My soldiers had brought in everyone who claimed to have seen a king's guard and a noblewoman. So far, every testimony had been useless, contradictory, and even far-fetched.

Theobald allowed himself a tight but mirthless smile. "I think you will be happy with this witness, Your Majesty."

He motioned to the guards to bring forward their prisoner. They prodded the captive with the tips of their swords until the prisoner collapsed to the floor near the dais. Wearing a gray robe with a hood, I couldn't see his face. Still, I could tell this was no ordinary citizen but rather a monk or priest belonging to one of the holy orders.

"A nun, Your Majesty," the captain explained. "I've been interviewing all the nuns left in Mercia."

I smiled at the cleverness of his plan. If any nuns knew what had happened at St. Cuthbert's, the captain's interviewing techniques would surely wrest that information from them. "Are they cooperating?"

"Quite well," Theobald said. "So much so that I have finally been led to this nun who was at St. Cuthbert's and has seen the princesses." The captain gave the woman a push with the tip of his boot.

The nun didn't react.

The captain's face tightened with barely restrained anger. He yanked off the nun's hood, heedless of the hair he tore from her head. She'd apparently lost her veil and wimple. Her shorn hair was matted to her head by blood and dirt. Her face was bruised and her body broken.

Clearly, the captain had already attempted to gain information from this woman.

I stepped down toward her. "Tell me, captain. What secrets has this nun exposed?"

"She's a stubborn one," Theobald said almost bitterly. "And she has insisted in speaking only to you."

I peered down at the bloody mass of what was left of the nun. I didn't condone violence against women, particularly women of the cloth who'd devoted their lives to serving God. However, I could not rebuke the captain for his use of torture in such a case as this. Not when the stakes were so high.

"What have you to say, Sister?" I asked.

She lifted her face then. Though the skin around her eyes was purple and swollen, her gaze was frank and piercing. "The royal princesses are lost to you." She spoke with an authority that took me by surprise. "They will remain lost, and you will not find them until the time is right for their return."

Theobald kicked the nun in the ribs, which caused her to cry out and double over. "You must address the king as 'Your Majesty.'"

I held up my hand to the captain, trying to quell the anxious premonition creeping up my spine. "Let her finish."

The captain nodded, stepped back, and crossed his hands behind his back.

After a moment, the nun pushed herself up. Though she seemed to struggle for consciousness, her voice was still strong. "The princesses will have Solomon's treasure to aid them, and there will be nothing you can do to stop them." She held me captive in a stare that stirred the foreboding deep inside me.

"Then you know the location of the keys to the ancient treasure?"

"The keys are lost to you as well." As she spoke the last word, she crumpled back to the floor, unconscious.

The captain grabbed a fistful of her hair and jerked her head up. "Tell the king all you know or you will die."

The nun's head slumped to the side. For this woman of the cloth, death would be a gift—a gift I would not grant her. "Do not kill her." I spun and retraced the steps to my throne. "I suspect she will prove more useful to us alive than dead."

The captain ordered his soldiers to lift the woman and carry her away.

"To the tower," I called.

Theobald nodded. "She will talk eventually and tell us everything we wish to know." He leaned in to the woman. "You can be sure of it, Sister Katherine. You can be sure."

Jody Hedlund is the best-selling author of over twenty historicals for both adults and teens and is the winner of numerous awards including the Christy, Carol, and Christian Book Award. She lives in central Michigan with her husband, five busy teens, and five spoiled cats. Learn more at JodyHedlund.com

Young Adult Fiction from Jody Hedlund

The Lost Princesses

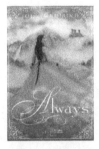

Always: Prequel Novella

On the verge of dying after giving birth to twins, the queen of Mercia pleads with Lady Felicia to save her infant daughters. With the castle overrun by King Ethelwulf's invading army, Lady Felicia vows to do whatever she can to take the newborn princesses and their three-year old sister to safety, even though it means sacrificing everything she holds dear, possibly her own life.

Evermore

Raised by a noble family, Lady Adelaide has always known she's an orphan. Little does she realize she's one of the lost princesses and the true heir to Mercia's throne . . . until a visitor arrives at her family estate, reveals her birthright as queen, and thrusts her into a quest for the throne whether she's ready or not.

Foremost and Hereafter coming soon . . .

The Noble Knights

The Vow

Young Rosemarie finds herself drawn to Thomas, the son of the nearby baron. But just as her feelings begin to grow, a man carrying the Plague interrupts their hunting party. While in forced isolation, Rosemarie begins to contemplate her future—could it include Thomas? Could he be the perfect man to one day rule beside her and oversee her parents' lands?

An Uncertain Choice

Due to her parents' promise at her birth, Lady Rosemarie has been prepared to become a nun on the day she turns eighteen. Then, shortly before her birthday, a friend of her father's enters the kingdom and proclaims her parents' will left a second choice—if Rosemarie can marry before the eve of her eighteenth year, she will be exempt from the ancient vow.

A Daring Sacrifice

In a reverse twist on the Robin Hood story, a young medieval maiden stands up for the rights of the mistreated, stealing from the rich to give to the poor. All the while, she fights against her cruel uncle who has taken over the land that is rightfully hers.

For Love & Honor

Lady Sabine is harboring a skin blemish, one, that if revealed, could cause her to be branded as a witch, put her life in danger, and damage her chances of making a good marriage. After all, what nobleman would want to marry a woman so flawed?

A Loyal Heart

When Lady Olivia's castle is besieged, she and her sister are taken captive and held for ransom by her father's enemy, Lord Pitt. Loyalty to family means everything to Olivia. She'll save her sister at any cost and do whatever her father asks—even if that means obeying his order to steal a sacred relic from her captor.

A Worthy Rebel

While fleeing an arranged betrothal to a heartless lord, Lady Isabelle becomes injured and lost. Rescued by a young peasant man, she hides her identity as a noblewoman for fear of reprisal from the peasants who are bitter and angry toward the nobility.

A complete list of my novels can be found at jodyhedlund.com.

Would you like to know when my next book is available? You can sign up for my newsletter, become my friend on Goodreads, like me on Facebook, or follow me on Twitter.

Newsletter: jodyhedlund.com
Goodreads: goodreads.com/author/show/3358829.Jody_Hedlund
Facebook: facebook.com/AuthorJodyHedlund
Twitter: @JodyHedlund

The more reviews a book has, the more likely other readers are to find it. If you have a minute, please leave a rating or review. I appreciate all reviews, whether positive or negative.

CPSIA information can be obtained
at www.ICGtesting.com
Printed in the USA
BVHW070413290820
587582BV00001B/242

9 781733 753401